BOWIE KNIFE

H. BEDFORD-JONES

BOWIE KNIFE

H. BEDFORD-JONES

COVER BY
V.E. PYLES

ALTUS PRESS • 2014

TABLE OF CONTENTS

CHAPTER I

"GOING TO TEXAS!"

HUGH KENLY was sitting over his rum in one corner, when snatches of the amazing talk got his attention. This catch-all groggery at one end of the New Orleans waterfront was miscalled the Hotel Beausejour; a rough and roaring place.

The night, of September, 1835, was thick and close; infernally so, thought Kenly. He was drinking down his heartsick disaster and loneliness. He was ripe for anything, careless of everything. The challenge of his brown eyes under shaggy brows, of his scarred, hard features, was surly. Heavy jaw, heavy hand, heavy heart. There was none in this guzzling, tobacco-chewing, smoking throng to discern any tender light in those brooding dark eyes, any softer touch of chivalry in his high-boned features. This night weighed upon him frightfully. It frightened him with old memories.

Thick outside and thick inside was the night. Outside, thick with heavy fog that rolled in off the river, up over the levee and the boats, to saturate everything with its swampy, viscous reek. Gutters dripped as with rain. Window lights and the glazed lanterns beaconing the hotel signs glimmered wanly like faces of drowning men. The black sky was low with moist warm air that had met chill river air, so that a man oozed sweat at every pore.

A sullen rumble, born of no apparent horizon, occasionally rolled through space. The air seemed weighted with a menace of quickening events, to Hugh Kenly.

Had he been up Missouri way, now, he would have been minded of earthquake. This thickness and closeness and rumbling had heralded the big quake along the river below St. Louis in the winter of 1811. Twenty-four years back—well, close to it. Kenly had been scant three years old, yet he remembered the terror of it, and had heard many yarns.

Yet this night registered memories far more poignant, more bitter, and more recent. Memories that caused him to reach again for the rum flask, with an oath.

Inside the groggery it was thick, not only with the fog but with fumes of twist tobacco, rum, whisky, dank clothing and bodies. It was murmurous with the undertones of men at drink and at confab. Undertones shot through with lightning of ribald oaths and wild, cocky whoops. Frenchmen, Americans, back-

"We'll tame you proper!"

woodsmen, rivermen, Spaniards, halfbreeds, their bodies steaming. And ever the word on all lips was the same: Texas!

Hugh Kenly grunted in disgust, and drained his mug. The ribs, recently mended, encasing his powerful lungs ached. The scars of his healed burns smarted and stung, and the fiery rum failed as medicine for either spirit or body. His only visible scar was the skinned triangle high on the bridge of his nose; a scar that marked him, however.

A steamboat mate without a berth, and with sharp memories. He thought of the snag that had driven through the hull of the *Amos G. Dunn*, exploding her boiler and lifting him halfway to shore with his ribs caved in and his hide scalded. As far as he knew, the steamboat was still hung up on that treacherous sawyer below old Natchez. He himself was still hung up in New Orleans, out of bandages at last, and out of hope to boot, scowling at the world.

A night like this, he mused, thick and clammy as this, with him taking a trick at the wheel on a forced run for a tie-up place. Then—the stars came again and fell and he was in the water. Not to blame for that sawyer, one minute under water, next minute above water; but they had blamed him all the same. Drunk, they had said. Drunk! The damned liars! Well, here was Hugh Kenly, none the less, heaving lead for soundings and finding none, except with the rum. Done for. Finished.

As a snag-end sawing up and down on the river surfaces catches the eye, so the smatterings of talk about him caught his ear. Texas, eh? Texas! There might be something in that, for a broken man. He listened deliberately, attentively.

"Land by the hundred of acres, I tell you, to be had freely!"

"But they say them Mexicans bears down on the settlers mortal bad."

"Cain't come it over Americans, you h'ar me orate? Who's to stop us?"

"No man's trail and every man's trail; that's the truth of it. Horses, trade goods, negroes... big profits in smuggling, lemme tell you! Lafitte lands slaves anywheres... trading with them Mexicans and—"

The voices died. Others took their places, striking Kenly's ear in curious sequence, unrelated apparently and yet with the snatches of talk rousing interest, provocative.

"Bound to declare for freedom, Americans won't stand being chiseled out'n their rights. No representation any more, and we ain't standing for it—"

"Volunteers... organizing to fight for Texas? Count me in, sure. Any gals for part of the plunder?"

And again, in more cultured tones curious to hear in such surroundings, yet impossible to assign to any certain speaker:

"I tell you, Santa Anna won't admit any state constitution. He's set himself up as dictator. Texas won't hear of such a thing. Now the settlers will have to go the whole hog and cut loose... aim at liberty. Liberty, understand?"

"Men enough in the United States to help her do it, too. We can't see our own blood ground down... new country thrown open. Mines, too, I hear. Silver mines...."

Provocative, yes, to a broken man. Kenly glanced around.

The room, murky with smoke and fog, was fairly large, its muddied plank floor occupied by chipped and stained deal tables crowded with sitters in leather, wool, and homespun. This was the front room of the two-storied hotel. Back along the hall extended other rooms devoted to sundry purposes, and on the second floor were lodgings. Hugh Kenly would not sleep here tonight, however. He was down to his last sou; or, in the local parlance, his last picayune.

Again and again his eyes drifted curiously to the table in that countering corner by this rear wall, beyond the threshold of the hallway. Three men sat there, bent forward in low and secretive poise. There were two profiles, and a back. Why they attracted him, Kenly did not know; unless it was that they were niched off there to themselves in a defensive manner. They appeared to be intent upon certain objects laid on the table, which they examined and discussed.

So intent was Kenly's gaze that it was noticed; the man of the back turned suddenly about and regarded Kenly with a cold, who-the-devil-are-you sort of stare. A slender man, yet muscular and square-shouldered, in short, lapelled jacket, linen roll collar and planter's black hat. The face leaped out at Kenly angrily.

A smooth countenance flanked by dark hair down either temple; a countenance marked by bold, challenging blue eyes. The straight nose and straight determined lips, the broad forehead, denoted plainly enough a masterful man, one who might be the noblest of friends and the deadliest of enemies. No one would forget him, and those stark blue eye's would forget no one.

IN HIS prickle of resentment under that blue stare, Kenly

was relieved by a more friendly salute, as a man came to his table and kicked out one of the stools, and spoke in soft Spanish.

"With your permission, *señor?* Good evening to you."

A Spaniard, this, or Mexican, enveloped in a serape; by his barb, of the lower class, with a strongly pockmarked face, yet not unpleasing. He had come with velvet step and seated himself with feline grace. Now he smiled on Hugh Kenly.

"You are alone, *señor?* You speak the Spanish?"

"A little," returned Kenly, by no means glad of the intrusion.

"*Bueno!* I thought you were alone, *señor.* You are not of these others; they are not your friends?" and the speaker swept his hand toward the room.

Kenly eyed him dourly. "I don't know them, nor you either."

"Good, good! Then you are not 'for Texas,' as their saying goes."

Kenly laughed curtly, savagely. "I'm for an honest job, *amigo.* Anywhere. If that's being for Texas, then I call the main, and devil take who likes it or doesn't!"

Unconsciously, his voice had lifted. Again the blue-eyed man had looked his way, other faces were turned. The pockmarked man leaned forward earnestly. He began to speak rapidly, as though rattling off something he had learned.

"I, too, am an honest man, *señor;* these people are fools. When they talk of Texas, to them it rains packsaddles. They think in miracles! *Señor,* Texas is a part of Mexico and remains so. Those *Americanos* who go in there to plunder and fight will be no more than outlaws, men without a country."

An ironic grunt broke from Kenly. "Maybe they'll take a country, my friend."

"Bah! The United States will not protect pirates who come from its own borders," rattled on the other. "Mexico will deal with them, and with all in Texas who rebel against her. There is a great man in Mexico now! Santa Anna is president and general, Mexico is now one people—and welcomes the brave and honest. What does your heart desire, *señor?* Money, honors, women? Listen, *señor*, a fire is discovered by its own light. Let me lead you to one who—*diablo!* Your servant, *señor*; we shall meet again, later—"

Even as he spoke, he was gone. Gone with the agile spring of a startled buck.

He disappeared into the hallway and was lost to sight. In his place loomed another figure, bulking out the smoky lights.

"Stranger, my compliments!"

With scrape of legs, the stool was again occupied, and Hugh Kenly stared at the taker. No Spaniard here. Quite the contrary, in fact.

A swart, black-haired, shrewd-eyed man, to be sure, but withal a beak-nosed man, Indian-visaged, in coonskin cap and fringed buckskin; a white man who carried a prodigiously long and silver-mounted rifle, leaning it against the table.

"Friend of your'n?" and he nodded in the direction of the vanished Mexican.

"First met, sir, the same as yourself," said Kenly, who was beginning to be amused. He was not certain whether to be angry or interested in this visitor; his amusement was apt to a swift and irritable change. Other faces were again turned in this direction.

"Meaning I'm barking up the wrong tree?" inquired this backwoodsman, with so ingratiating and honest a smile that Kenly's irritation melted.

"I wouldn't say that," he rejoined. "You're welcome to poor company if you like it, stranger."

"As the coon in the tree said to the hound in the canebrake," observed the other, with a whimsical twitch of his long, square chin. "Well, I expect poor company may be better than none, seeing as you just had it afore I come. I don't ask you to kick afore you're spurred, but we may's well go straight ahead. I'm delegated to inquire how you are on the G.T.T., stranger."

"Gone to Texas, eh?" Kenly had picked up enough talk to know what these initials meant in local parlance. "Well, my friend, you can see for yourself. I haven't gone." The other chuckled.

"Neat as a possum's tail. That's sufficient, as Tom Haynes said when he saw the elephant. You don't need to cover up on me, stranger. I'm Davy Crockett from Tennessee, seeing the sights with Betsy, here," and he patted the long rifle affectionately. "Not gone to Texas—Going To Texas! There's a motto to hang on your door, blast my old shoes if it ain't! You're a likely feller; what d'you say? Another horn of liquor, and the honor's mine! Will you crack the heads of a few dons for the sake of liberty?"

CROCKETT FROM Tennessee? Hugh Kenly had heard the name; everyone had heard of the deadly shooting Tennesseean.

"Well, why not?" he answered. "I'm flattened out and open to a berth of any paying kind. What's the offer?"

"To go with me to Texas," said Crockett.

"With you?" Kenly's dark eyes lit up suddenly.

"Right you are," said Crockett. "Dog me if I don't know a man when I see one! I'm here to talk with Jim Bowie and get the news. He's busy right now, but I'll fetch him over when he comes back. He's a high-toned gentleman, fresh out of Texas, and can argufy with you better'n Davy Crockett, any day."

Crockett stretched out his legs comfortably. Kenly had him spotted now. One of the three men from that corner table. He glanced over at it, and found the table empty. The man with the hot blue eyes had disappeared.

"Y'know," went on Crockett, "Jim's the popularist man in that there country, and a screamer in a fight. The way he laid into them Injuns when he was looking for his silver mine was something to holler about."

"Silver mine?" repeated Hugh Kenly, blankly.

"Yep. Somewhere in Texas. He's rich enough already, but it'll make him richer than a congressman if he can find it again," and Crockett exploded in a laugh. "Me, I been in congress, and the most I got out of it was a trip on them new railroad cars.

Seventeen mile in fifty-five minutes—yes, sir! Hell in harness, as the feller said when his horses run away. Well, what was I talking about?"

"Jim Bowie."

"Oh, sure! Him and his mine. The cowards would give a pretty penny to get the gouge holt on that mine! But Jim'll talk Texas to you till the trail's as plain as a b'ar's path in a canebrake. If you want to travel with Davy Crockett, you and me can 'list in the cause of liberty together."

"If I want to!" exclaimed Kenly eagerly. "Why, Colonel Crockett, I—"

At this instant he heard a scream, echoing down the dark hallway.

There had been other voices of womankind, voices both gay and angry, bruited through these entertainment-precincts of the shaggy little hotel. These ribaldries had been an accepted feature of the evening. But this single note of frantic appeal startled him—though no one else seemed to notice it.

Kenly leaped to his feet, darted into the hall, and went plunging along, guided only by the threads of light glimmering through the cracks of the warped and loosely fitted doors to either hand. At the hall's end, however, there was a broader slant of yellow light that beckoned him on.

As he sped away, he heard roars of laughter from the big room behind, at some sally from Davy Crockett. Then he heard sounds ahead, also. His senses focused upon the scuffle and stamp of feet, the gusty oaths and laughs of men, the quick desperate cries of a woman. All coming from that slant of light, as though it were a signal of distress.

The door stood ajar, and coming to it, Kenly shouldered it aside and burst in.

The room, as revealed by a tipsy lamp in a wall bracket, was in a wild disorder of upset table and stools. All in a flashing glance, Hugh Kenly caught the full gist of it. The Spaniard with the pockmarked face lying senseless in one corner; an old woman, huddled against the wall and piping frantically. Two men wrestling with and wresting at a young woman—one man leather-capped, in greasy river-jerkin, a faded kerchief knotted about his neck; the other a blazing carrot-thatch, cursing furiously.

Then Kenly saw the woman, young, of bright hair and pale angry lips parted over clenched teeth. Her upper dress was torn. Her hand gripped a knife, but carrot-thatch held it high and useless as she strained and fought the two men.

"The she-devil! Gouge her!"

"We'll tame you proper—"

"*Señor*, help, help me!" shrilled her voice, as she saw Kenly there in the doorway.

The straight appeal was explanation enough; the answer was swift.

Kenly's right arm crooked about the kerchief and throat of the jerkined man, his bent knee jammed into the fellow's spine. To a drag and a twist, the rascal went reeling to fall all asprawl outside the doorway. Kenly caught up a stool for weapon, but stood holding it.

For, her knife-hand released, the young woman lashed out viciously. A wild oath burst from carrot-thatch; then, his retreat cut off by Kenly, he went headfirst through the crashing window.

"Behind you, *señor*—behind you!"

THE WOMAN'S voice brought Kenly around, stool in hand. Things were dim and dazed. The room wavered in the flickers of the draft-blown lamp. The woman, the shadows, the lust of combat, the thick dust from the stamped floor, were in his eyes.

That looming figure in the doorway—the man he had flung out, of course! Kenly leaped, and the stool in his hand whirled.

"What's the matter in here—"

The voice was keen and hard, level, impetuous. It died out

under the crash of the heavy stool, as the edge of the wood thudded home.

Too late, too late! Kenly could not halt the blow, though he realized his mistake in that frightful moment. Nor could the swiftly uplifted arm of the other man parry it. For an instant Kenly recoiled under the stabbing blaze of those stark blue eyes. Something clattered and fell across the floor, from that upflung arm. Then the intruder pitched forward, full length, to lie face down and without movement.

"He has it! He has it!" The cry came from the young woman. "Now we must be quick, quick!"

She hurled herself forward, caught at the door, slammed it shut and ran home the bar. Then she whirled around.

Outside and in had fallen silence, save for the rapid panting of the younger woman as she eyed Kenly, and the babblings of the crone huddled in fear and trembling against the wall.

The lamp had steadied now. Its flame rose full and bright. Kenly's vision came clear again. He could scarce believe her real, in this his first intelligent view of her. Shaken over her shoulders, her hair gleamed like silken floss of gold. Her wide eyes were the hue of the bluebird at mating time, her lips were vivid red, her skin was very white, and soft to the sight. She was all whiteness, softness, ruddy tenderness, save for the knife that glittered cold in her hand. No less a woman than a girl.

"Ah, *señor*, thanks, a thousand thanks!" Her breath still came fast, her breasts were heaving under the torn, rent stuff of her gown. "These ruffians, these Americans, they would have—ah, Matilde! Quick! And you, *señor*—we must go, we must go before those others return. Matilde!"

This to the crone, who now scrambled forward hurriedly.

"A thousand curses on them!" she breathed. "Look at the pretty stone—this one, that fell from his hand! So he would pay us by throwing it at my feet, eh?" And hideous laughter cackled from her lips, as she gathered up a bit of rock from the floor. It was this that had clattered down, ere the intruder fell.

Swiftly, the girl flung herself upon the prostrate figure, while Kenly stared.

"True, true! He may have more, then. Help me, *señor!* Help me turn him over, before others come. Search him, Matilde!"

Kenly lent a hand. They turned the still figure upon its back, and the features stared up at them with bold and fixed blue eyes. The eyes, and the deadly, oozing bruise upon the uncovered forehead! Kenly started back with a sudden chill from the look of those accusing eyes, eyes well remembered, eyes that had not forgotten. Yes, this was the man of the blue eyes, the fine garments, the hat that now lay crushed on the floor. Then Kenly felt the girl clutch his arm.

"You have killed him, *señor*; no time now—with me, quickly, or you also are dead. Make haste, Matilde."

The crone, Matilde, had made deft and swiftly accomplished search. Now she tottered up from her knees with a wild flutter of old laughter.

"The very man indeed, my pet. A knife, tucked under his shirt. This bit of paper. A few coins. I thought so great a man would be richer by far. The knife for you, *señor?*"

Mechanically, Hugh Kenly accepted the heavy knife thrust into his hand.

"I did not mean to strike him down," he muttered, stammering out the words. I thought he was the other—"

SUDDENLY HIS senses, still dulled by the rum, awoke. He became aware of breaking tumult outside; voices were sounding, feet were trampling, and there came a hammering thud of fists at the door, with deep resounding shouts to open.

"With me, *señor!*" The girl caught at his arm. Kenly looked at her.

"Where?"

"I'll show you. Come."

"But this man here?" He indicated the senseless Mexican of

the pockmarked face, the man who had spoken to him at the table.

"Bah! Only a peon. Leave him for them to kill."

"I will not"

The girl had snatched up a cloak and was throwing it around her shoulders. The old woman had darted to an unseen, flush, small door in the farther side of the room, a door contrived for secret use. Matilde disappeared, the girl following hurriedly.

Leave the man for them to kill? With a grunt, Kenly stooped and lifted. For some reason he liked that pockmarked fellow. The man was half conscious. At first he feebly resisted, then lent himself to the effort. He got the man through the little door, and instantly the girl, who was waiting, slammed and locked it.

"Follow!"

Somehow he stumbled through the darkness with the weight of pock-face, and emerged into a muddy lane, thick with the moist night and the fog.

The flitting glimmer of the girl's white ankles below her cloak could just be seen. This, and the stressed whinneys of the crone, whose legs were better than her lungs, provided guidance. Their steps were sped by the growing, gathering clamor of voices and angry shouts behind.

The lane was long and crooked. It brought them into a street. Save for the few sickly lights above entrance ways and behind dingy panes, the street was dark and lifeless. The girl, with the crone at her heels, led on, brushing close against the fronting buildings while her slippers clicked upon the cobbles.

Abruptly, she turned into an entrance, her cloak whipping from sight beneath the grilled light. The old woman scuttled after, nimbly enough. Kenly followed, only half-supporting the supposed Spaniard, who was manfully working his legs now.

A paved court was overlooked by a railed balcony, soft lights burning dimly. Kenly followed the others up a stairway which brought him to the balcony. Ahead, the girl had halted at a door scrolled with iron-work, rapping repeatedly, quickly.

"It is I, Rodrigo! Open, open!"

The door flung back, and she slipped through upon a shaft of light. The hag followed. Kenly guided in his peon, and as he did so, the girl shut the door and shot a bolt.

"Well, my cousin, all is over," said the girl calmly. She caught up a chair, brought it over to the fire, and seated herself, thrusting soggy slippers to the blaze. "Heavens, what an escape!"

Then she burst into laughter, as Kenly stood gaping at the scene which met his eye.

CHAPTER II

THE MAP

I T WAS, indeed, a strange scene that greeted Hugh Kenly, by contrast to that which he had so recently left. Yet he was not the only one to stand in staring surprise.

In New Orleans, this city half-Spanish and half-French, such a room was not uncommon, with its glittering old furniture, carved tables, ornate chandelier, dressed cowhide rugs upon the floors and heavy brocaded curtains covering the windows. In a wide hearth blazed a warm and ruddy fire, grateful to see despite the steaming moisture of the night; its warmth, at least, was good honest warmth. The cloudy marble mantlepiece held various knickknacks.

On the central table was a tray of food, with glasses and a large decanter of wine.

The duenna, if such were the old crone, huddled at one side of the fireplace, babbling thanks to the saints. The peon, for he seemed to be rather a peon of humble birth than any proud Spaniard, leaned against the wall. Kenly caught his mumble.

"I will remember, *señor*. You have saved me; I will remember."

The American paid no heed, for he was looking at the startled man, surprised by their abrupt entry.

This man had been seated at a writing desk against the wall. He, very obviously, was a true Spaniard. A man of thirty, well-favored, albeit of eyes a little close, of ruddy olive complexion, aquiline features, thin-bridged nose. His black mustache turned up from full lips, his chin was deeply cleft, and curly black hair framed his visage. He wore an embroidered black velvet jacket over a fine linen shirt, a yellow waist sash, and boots of soft leather, fancifully stitched, coming above the knees. A fine fellow, this Spaniard, and his black eyes reminded Kenly of the knife still in his hand.

The soft laughter of the girl broke upon the silence.

"Well, Rodrigo, you might ask the *señor* to sit down! I do not have his name, so introductions must wait. You are not hospitable, good cousin! What, food and wine to hand, and you offer us none, when this *señor* has saved us all?"

She laughed again, as in soft mockery. She had stowed her hair in a glossy pile, and now sat, luxurious as a basking cat, all unconcerned over her torn upper garment. She was not unmindful of certain effects, as Kenly could dimly sense.

The man Rodrigo was obviously disconcerted by Kenly's presence, a prey to awkward uncertainty. At these words from the girl, he seemed to recollect himself. He bowed, and spoke with a certain stiffness.

"Your pardon, Conchita. And yours, *señor*. Surprise, I fear, caused by my unintentional rudeness. Will you be pleased to sit down, *señor*? Before the fire; it is yours. At least it banishes the dampness of this fog-ridden night. For the love of the saints, Pablo, do quit rubbing your head like a jackass against a wall, and take a seat. Pour wine, Matilde."

About the man was a briskness, a hearty quality, which invited no denial.

"Yes, my captain," Pablo faltered. He gingerly perched on the edge of a chair and held his head between his hands. An aching, thrumming head, no doubt. The old woman began to pour wine from the decanter into the glasses.

Kenly, with a nod, seated himself at the end of the fireplace opposite the girl. She fascinated him. This warmth was grateful to his aching ribs; but the warmth that pervaded him was not all from the fire.

The girl—Conchita, the Spaniard had called her—threw

glances at him. Her hands arranged stray tendrils of her hair with deft touches, her eyes insisted that he appraise her. Above small slippers, her ankles were slender and shapely. The flash of her white skin, the lovely curve of her cheek and throat, the slight smile resting upon those red lips, the deep blue of her eyes framed in long lashes and crescent brows, the amazing pile of amber sunset hair—yes, she was worth looking at, this girl.

Hugh Kenly became conscious of his harsh garb of riverman. He bethought himself to lay down the knife and cover it with his hat; it was out of place here, at a hearth which seemed domestic.

A suspense was in the air, a sensation of waiting, as though no one dared be the first to speak. Matilde was handing about the glasses of wine. Rodrigo pulled up a chair and seated himself. The girl took her glass. She poised it, with glance aside and the quick, half-mocking utterance: "To Mexico, *señor!*" She brought the glass to her lips, a smile flashing forth at Kenly.

He tasted the wine, making no other reply. The tang of the rich, molten gold was grateful to his throat. The smile from her lips warmed him, permeated him with a friendliness, a promise of cheer. Then, abruptly, the wrinkled old woman shattered the silence with her senile, evil twitter.

"There, my captain; I wiped every glass with my skirt. You can trust old Matilde! I was not well brought up for nothing. And now see what I have for you; it will gladden your heart, my captain! Here, from my pocket; this, and this. You see the treasure, my captain? I cannot read the paper, but I know what it is, and I can read the pretty stone, for that talks plainly enough."

Thus saying, she fished out the piece of rock and the folded square of paper taken from the dead man, if indeed he were dead. She laid them under Rodrigo's nose and stood back triumphant, a grin splitting her toothless face.

"What the devil! What nonsense is here, you old witch?" broke out the captain, his wine still untasted. "There is much to explain, true, but you make a poor beginning. Come, Conchita! What is the meaning of all this absurdity?"

Matilde took the word and bristled.

"Absurdity indeed!" she squawked out in shrill anger. "I have just told you the wine won't poison you, and neither will these things. If the captain will finger the rock and look into the paper, he will count this night the most blessed of his life. He calls me names, eh? Well, one who finds he cannot bite should not show his teeth."

SUCH SAYINGS were the stock in trade of all Spanish folk. Don Rodrigo grunted in response, and turned the rock over in his hand. He put teeth to it and wiped his lips. He examined into the paper, and sat back in his chair, frowning.

"Well, devil take you! What's the answer?"

"*Plata bruta*—pure ore of silver," and old Matilde almost snarled the words in her excitement. "And that paper should be a map,"

"Well? What of it?" demanded the other, staring at her.

"What of it? The mines of San Saba lie in your hand, little general, and you say what of it?" Shrill laughter put mockery into her words. "I know. I have had ore like this in my hands before; but not enough to fill a cart. Anyway, both the ore and the map come from the right place, the right man. It is San Saba silver—is it not, my little one?"

She turned, appealing swiftly to the girl, who merely shrugged and nodded.

"San Saba! The San Saba mines? Holy saints!" Now excitement seized upon the captain, and no mistake. He tossed off his wine and thrust the glass on the table. "I do not believe it. You are trying to jest with me, all of you—come! Let's have an explanation of all this—who is this *señor*, whence come this ore and paper?"

Without pause for answer, he turned to Kenly.

"*Señor*, pardon my remissness. I am Captain Don Rodrigo

Estremadura. The lady is my cousin, Doña Maria de la Concepcion Villamar. And you?"

"My name is Kenly—Hugh Kenly. Hugo, in the Spanish."

"Ah, Hugo!" exclaimed Doña Maria, mouthing it prettily as she leaned forward. "It is a brave, harsh name, well fitting a brave man. A brave man is known by his deeds and his scars—a true *caballero*, my Hugo!"

"Curse your fine phrases!" exclaimed Don Rodrigo, riding the saddle of impatience. "Tell me what happened, do you hear? To the story, and quickly."

"Why, my cousin, two men attacked me—"

"Where was this?"

"In the room at the hotel. Where else? You should know very well."

"What!" cried Don Rodrigo. "I ordered that only one man should be brought to you at a time. How was this, Pablo? You dared to disobey me?"

"Pardon, my captain," said the pock-faced Pablo. "The two *Americanos* were friends and in company. They said it was both or none—how could I prevent them?"

"You're a fool. All right, Conchita; go on."

Doña Maria shrugged. "They struck Pablo down. They were not so much for Mexico as for a pretty face, it proved. They had drunk heavily, and they were ruffians."

One hand touched her knife significantly.

"Two ruffians and using force, you comprehend. And then came Don Hugo. He alone paid heed to my scream; in that place, no one cares what happens. He is a man indeed; He picked up one and actually hurled him out! The other fled through the window. Then in walked a third, and him Don Hugo left lying on the floor with a cracked skull, dead. Beautifully dead, Rodrigo! A pretty blow."

Kenly shivered slightly at her tone, at the memory. That mistaken blow irked him.

"And the pretty stone for proof," cackled old Matilde. "Right at my feet the fine *señor* threw it, for safekeeping while he slept. May he never waken!"

"But the map?" rapped out Don Rodrigo.

"Oh, he gave us that also," and the crone chuckled. "And a fine knife to Don Hugo."

"Plague take you!" broke out Don Rodrigo angrily. "Be done with your cursed riddles; I've no time to bother with them. Speak plainly! Who were the two men?"

"Ruffians, my cousin," said Doña Maria. She spoke now with an Andalusian lisp, which obviously irritated Don Rodrigo. "No matter; they were not for us in any case, though I should have liked to mark them with my knife—"

"The third? He of the map, of this ore?"

"Your wits are slow tonight, Rodrigo. Who should he be, but Don Santiago Bowie?"

"Exactly," and Matilde put in her cackle. "The fine gentleman of the San Saba mines, the rich man, the politician—grr! May he rot in hell!"

"Jim Bowie? That man? No, no! It could not be—"

Kenly's voice rose in wild force as he sprang to his feet, his chair falling back, his wineglass tinkling and shivering on the hearth. The wine spread red like blood at his feet. He stood wide-eyed, astounded, dismayed, a paralysis seizing upon him.

"You did not know?" The girl's brows lifted as she eyed him. "*Dios*, what a blow you struck! It would have killed an ox. What matter? You are safe with us."

"DEAD? THIS *señor* killed that man, that Hercules?" exclaimed Don Rodrigo, no less aghast than Kenly himself. Then his dark eyes warmed, and a smile of delight rushed to his full lips. "The greatest fighter of all the border—dead! This will be good news for *El Presidente*, Señor Bui, dead!" He gave the name its usual pronunciation, alike in both Spanish and English. "The Bowie of the San Saba mines, the traitor to

Mexico—and he has given us the mines! Oh, a great stroke, Señor Kenly, and Mexico will reward you well!"

"Bowie!" muttered Kenly. "A traitor, you say? But he was no Mexican."

"But yes," and Don Rodrigo nodded. "A Mexican citizen, *amigo*, like all those who settled in Texas. Pablo! You knew the man. Are you certain it was Bowie?"

The pock-marked Pablo looked up and assented. "Yes, my captain; I did not see him dead, but I knew him in life. He had been in the tavern room, with two other men, examining bits of rock. I said to myself then that it might be a matter of the San Saba treasure; but Don Santiago would be carrying his name-knife."

The knife—the famous type invented by Bowie's brother? The ore and the map? The man at the table with Crockett, those challenging, hot blue eyes? Hugh Kenly groped for his chair again and sank down in it. He saw it all now, with horrible precision. Bowie showing the ore, talking with those other two men. Then the scream, and Bowie, the famous chivalric Bowie, to the room, still holding the ore in his hand. The convulsive release of the ore when the blow fell. A shiver ran through Kenly, a shiver of repulsion, of self-horror. Not at death. He was used to that on the river. But at the hideous mistake which had caused him to kill a man famed throughout the southwest for his noble chivalry no less than for his dreaded fighting ability.

The girl was speaking, and her musing words sank into him.

"Jeem Bowie, yes. I have seen him often enough. Everyone in San Antonio de Bejar knows Jeem Bowie. Did he not marry one of the Veramendi girls, whose father was vice-governor? And he had cotton mills in the south, until cholera carried off his wife and children. A Mexican citizen, of course. Don Hugo, have no fear! Mexico will thank you for ridding her of this traitor, this man who calls himself a Texan."

"That is well said, my heart," commended Don Rodrigo, with

a nod of approval. "This Bowie left Bejar to join the plotters here, raising men and money; he was not here for his San Saba mines alone." A short laugh broke from him, as his keen black eyes leaped to the American.

"I do not ask, Señor Kenly, what your own plans may have been; whether you were for the Texas rebels or not, is immaterial now. You are, you must be, to Mexico with us. That is to say, to, Bejar. There you are safe, honored, a hero!"

"I have already invited the *caballero* to listen to us, my captain," proffered the pock-marked Pablo. "I was about to take him back to the room to see Doña Maria and talk with her, but another intervened. Then I picked up those ruffians, and they rushed along with me—"

"Never mind," and Don Rodrigo waved his hand airily. "Señor Kenly, matters have turned out well for you, marvelously well! There are great things ahead for you. We have many Americans in our army, from generals to drill-sergeants. But for you, also, there are now things to be avoided, since you have killed Jim Bowie, a man of note among his people.

"He has brothers and friends; you cannot go back to that hotel, you cannot venture into the streets. You cannot stay in this part of the United States, and you will assuredly be safe among Americans in Texas. For, *señor*, pardon my reference, but you are a marked man. You bear a scar upon your nose which is unusual, impossible to conceal. Well! Mexico will not only offer you protection, but honors and wealth. *Señor*, to your health."

And Don Rodrigo drained his glass, which old Matilde had refilled. The crone uttered her evil twittering laugh, so shot through with venom, with vindictive malice, that the recurrent sound of its mirth sent a chill down Kenly's spine. He sat there with hopeless realization growing upon him, liking his company less every moment and yet fully conscious that Don Rodrigo spoke the truth.

"The great Don Santiago brought low!" cackled the old

woman. "One who they say rode alligators like horses, and picked his teeth with a knife as long as my arm. Ha! Toothless as a cock now is he, but one who was dreaded while living may well be feared after he is dead, my fine *señor* of the marked nose!"

"Shut up," snapped Don Rodrigo. "*Señor*, let us look at this map together. You may help me with this American writing—"

KENLY ROSE, wakening his sluggard faculties. The captain had pulled up a small table. With heavy head and heavy heart, Kenly joined him there.

His brain was racing the while. How swiftly things had happened; how incredible that he should have killed Jim Bowie, even stricken him down! Jim Bowie, of the brothers made forever popular and respected by their bowie-knife, made more famous by valiant deeds of a kind dear to common talk and hearts!

Kenly saw that he was not to join Davy Crockett on the Texas road. He had sat alone and aloof; he had been observed and regarded suspiciously. The covert Pablo had approached him. Then Crockett, quickly, to sound him out. Opportunity, in that scream, had been wrested from him. And now Bowie, found struck down and rifled, mayhap dead as the girl said! Those two other men in the room would know him again. Damnation, what a coil! Whether or not for Texas, now he was for himself, in deadly peril, and a marked man. Crockett had eyed him well, and those shrewd eyes would know him under any disguise.

Beside Don Rodrigo he bent over the map, translated the few English words and terms showing there. A map carefully drawn, that came clear enough to the eye under the exclamations of the worthy captain.

"Now I see it plainly; look you, Señor Kenly," he said, tracing with well-kept finger; a finger somewhat blunted, but with spade-nail trimmed and polished. "A cross, here. Las Minas de Nuevo Almagres or in your tongue the new Almagres Mines.

Plain enough. And here the Rio San Saba—creek, it says, eh? The old San Saba mission should be somewhere about. Here mountains, and the trail from Bejar; by marches, seventy leagues. Two hundred miles or so—*pouf!* A mere nothing to hard legs. The ore speaks for itself." He leaned back and looked up at Kenly. "You know of the New Almagres mines, *amigo?*"

Kenly frowned. "Seems to me I heard something about it at Natchez, quite a while back. Some Injun fight, wasn't it?"

"Precisely. Four years ago, in 1831; a famous battle, *señor*, and famous mines. They are almost pure silver, and had been worked by the viceroys of Spain. Miners from Almagres, Mexico, were sent to work them under protection of the San Saba mission, there on the river of the same name, in the Apache country."

"Apaches? I've heard a lot about that," Kenly said, "from the Santa Fe traders at St. Louis. They're devils, by all accounts."

"Devils; may God preserve us from them!" and the good captain signed himself furtively. "Yes. Those red devils, who prefer their patron to God, killed all the miners and put the mission to fire and knife. The mines were lost for many years, the Indians closing all that country. But our Santiago Bowie came into Texas on filibuster business; Lafitte the pirate was his partner, and to better affairs he turned good citizen of Mexico. He had found those mines again, he said, and he led a party of Americans into the Indian country to open them up."

Don Rodrigo twisted his trim mustache and gestured suavely.

"Well, they came back again," he pursued. "He and his party, bringing no silver at all, lucky to bring their lives. Not yet were those mines for Señor Bowie! Now, it is well known to us of Bejar, to General Cos and others, that the valorous *señor* was about to try again. Thanks to the Americans, the Indians are not so strong as once they were. But those mines are not for Texas and the rebellious Texans. They are for Mexico. *Caspita!* We must go and go at once. You comprehend?"

"We?" Kenly echoed.

"We," and Don Rodrigo smiled. With a gesture of finality, of decision, he folded up the map and pocketed it, with the bit of ore. "The map is ours, the ore is ours; there lies ahead only the trail. You, *señor*, are guest of honor, aid, assistant, friend. You will not be lonely in the service of Mexico, of *El Presidente*, I promise you! If these rebels are raising men, why, so are we. Riflemen, American recruits, to fight fire with fire! Here, Pablo. Your report. You had success?"

The pock-face stood up, with a shambling salute and a grin. Kenly found himself liking the fellow once more. Something resolute and honest and shrewd in that brown, pocked face. Good, sure eyes.

"Yes, my captain. Of those we had seen before, and one or two new ones. As Doña Maria will tell you, we sent them on to the boat. All will not come who promised, of course, but there will be some at least."

"S O I T is to be hoped. Go you, at once, and see that the way is clear and those aboard the boat ready. We shall leave immediately. Thanks be to the saints, our affairs here in New Orleans cause no delay! You, Matilde, pack the few things of ours which have not gone to the boat, and pay our bill here at this place. As for you, Don Kenly—"

"And as for me," broke in Doña Maria, with a silvery laugh, "I think we may all have a bit more wine. Pity to waste good wine, Rodrigo. Besides, our friend here does not comprehend. There are questions in his eyes. Eh, *señor?*"

"Questions, yes," replied Kenly, frowning slightly. "I don't quite understand it, why I should go, what is there for me. I'm not worried about the rights of it; but fighting against my own people—that's different."

"Ah, no, no!" exclaimed the girl impulsively. "That is not it. Come, Rodrigo; there is no haste to be off. Come, explain to our good *señor*, who has done so much for us!"

Rodrigo nodded, produced a small cigar, and lighted it at a candle. Kenly found his chair again, and the fire, and accepted the glass the girl handed him. She touched her own to it with a little clink. "To the tomorrow!" she murmured, but with her eyes she said; "To our tomorrow!" She seated herself, sipping the wine, with sidelong glances at the two men.

"You shall go with us to Bejar, *amigo*," said Don Rodrigo. "There is no other way, no better way, for you. I am on the staff of General Cos, commanding at San Antonio of Texas. What am I doing here in New Orleans, and Doña Maria? We are doing what so many Texans are doing, recruiting—but our recruits are for Mexico. We have more to offer, eh, Conchita?"

He broke into a laugh, then his gaze came back to Kenly.

"My friend, Mexico welcomes good citizens. On all who obey her laws she bestows land, privileges, and beautiful women who can be very kind if one has the right touch. Yes, *señor*, we have place for Americans who help us. As for the rebel Texans, what of them?" and he shrugged lightly. "Men without a country, once they rebel. How can they fight Mexico—eight million people, two hundred and fifty thousand soldiers, with the valiant Santa Anna to lead us? And with the savages on their own borders!"

"But are they fighting?" said Kenly, cutting with his cold prosaic query into the bombastic speech. "Fighting has not begun?"

"Even now, perhaps; at any moment the fools may begin! Texas is like the donkey of many owners. The Americans there dispute and fight among themselves. Many among them know that this cause, born of ingratitude, is hopeless. Here, let me read you what one of them says—a *pronunciamento* by Don John Williams—a man of good sense and standing, not one of the riffraff who invite the firing squad!"

From the desk against the wall, Don Rodrigo plucked a printed sheet, moved a candle closer, and read in his precise, clipped English.

"The yawning jaws of a hopeless war... so daring, so ungrateful, and so unprovoked... to protect the frontiers, to sustain our position against the combined forces of the Mexican United States—O Vanity! O Ignorance! The prey of political jugglers—"

"You see what your own people think?" The reader tucked away the paper with a graceful gesture. "The Texans who so foolishly take up arms will lose all—all! It will not be a war, however. We do not ask that you fight against your own people, *amigo*. We seek you, not as a fighter, but as one to deserve gratitude, as one who gives a great gift, here!" and he slapped the pocket which held the map and the bit of ore.

Kenly reflected grimly that he had not given either one. This don was too slick altogether, too glib with his words; yet he was a man to win respect. Now the girl leaned forward. Her voice came softly, warmly, as though for Kenly's ear alone.

"Ah, my Don Hugo! You will find all this and more to be the truth, when we see Bejar. There lies your future, my friend!"

"Assuredly," spoke Don Rodrigo, with his air of grand courtesy. "We take you to Bejar for your own safety, *caballero*. I have shown you how things are in Texas, were you already inclined that way. Further, we owe you a debt for your rescue of Doña Maria from those pigs who attacked her.

"Here you are in peril, in Bejar you are safe, honored. Mexico will be generous with brave gentlemen who serve the tricolor. Lands, bounty, honor, love of women, position! You wish land? *Pouf!* A grant of a thousand, ten thousand, acres is nothing! You understand, I speak freely; your interests and those of Mexico are the same. I'll take you to General Cos, where we may speak again of these silver mines you've given us."

Now the pock-faced Pablo made hasty entrance. "All clear, my captain! The inn is like a beehive with stings out, but the streets are quiet. I cannot answer for the recruits. They have not all come to the boat. Some have come and then gone away to get more liquor—"

"No matter." Don Rodrigo rose. "We bring Mexico what is more important than men—money! The richest silver mines in

the world! Your pardon, *amigo*; I must get my things together.
Conchita, dress quickly!"

He caught up belt and pistols, began to ram papers into a
portfolio. The girl slipped quietly out of the room.

Kenly sat there fingering the knife he had drawn from
beneath his hat. No doubt one of those bowie-knives of which
he had heard, invented by Rezin Bowie, brother of the man he
had struck down. Heavy, razor-edged, the point tipped upward
in a curve, of great length. The haft was crudely inlaid with
massive silver. Altogether, a most distinctive knife, one in a
thousand. Jim Bowie's knife! He shivered again at thought of
those blue, magnetic eyes, all astare in death.

Well he knew how to discount the honeyed words of Don
Rodrigo. Yet, though he could shed them, they held enough
truth to burn deeply into him. He had little or no choice in the
matter. And why not? As he knew, the Mexican army, Mexico
itself, was the happy hunting ground of American backwoods-
men, soldiers, gentlemen. His fingers closed on the inlaid haft
of the knife.

"You will come, Hugo *mio?*" The girl, now more darkly clad,
a cloak bound around her figure, had reappeared and was
coming to his side, her hand upon his arm like a caress. She
was very close to him; he could feel the glow of her, the warm
friendliness. He doubted it, he misliked her overt appeal, yet
she was not to be denied.

"Don Hugo!" The elegant Rodrigo was fastening a long cloak
about his throat, and spoke brusquely, with military authority.
"Do you come with us?"

"Aye," said Kenly. He had found himself now, had come to
a decision. It was his one chance, his only hope. Fortune drew
him, bright eyes, the future that lay over the horizon. A laugh
came to his lips, and his brown eyes lit up. "Aye, cap'n! I'm with
you, right enough."

"Good!" Don Rodrigo clapped him heartily on the shoulder.
"Matilde?"

"Ready and waiting, my captain," said Pablo. "I'll answer for her valise."

"Forward, then. I'll follow. *Señor*, will you bring Doña Maria? The rearguard to you, the post of honor!"

CHAPTER III

MATT DEVORE

KENLY FELT the girl's hand on his arm, hugged it against his breast, met her smile with a quick, eager laugh. The repressed vitality of him leaped forth, the energy in his brown, aquiline visage. Well or ill, he was for Texas now, sure enough!

A rear hall led them through the building. Dim lights, but the hand and tongue of the girl guided Kenly. Now down a stair or two, a rear balcony opened before them, and stairs descending into the open of a rear court. Thence, by an iron gate, unlighted, into the pent darkness of a thickly misted lane. The foggy mist was as wet as a drizzle.

The lane cut through into a street. A bracketed light, pale as a phantom, marked the exit. The girl was light but firm upon the American's arm; she was panting a little, more with eagerness and excitement than with effort. Kenly divined the quick, passionate spirit of her; at the moment it thrilled him, though at the back of his head he was not so sure about this tiger-girl.

So they made exit into the street. Pablo and Matilde were well in the lead. Don Rodrigo had fallen back, just ahead of Kenly and the girl. Scarcely did they set foot on the banquette when a voice leaped out.

"Stand! Halt, thar!"

The challenge was swift and sharp as a knife-thrust. There were three men with a lantern, materializing from a sunken doorway, blocking the path, pressing in, peering by the light of their lantern. The exultant cry of wolves at the kill pealed up.

"It's the Spanish girl! And the man, by the 'Tarnal—the very man!"

"Over goes their apple cart—take 'em, boys—"

Even in the rush of bodies and grappling hands, the scene changed, plunged into obscurity. With flutter of cloak and shrewd, agile kick, Don Rodrigo shivered the lantern; his clubbed pistol rose and fell. Kenly was clutched. By riverman's trick his boot heel impacted on a knee of the man who grappled him. The fellow lurched half about and pitched down, floundering in the slime.

A cry from Doña Maria, a savage, exultant cry. A wild oath, a scream; her knife had driven home. Two more figures had loomed out of the fog, hurling themselves into the fight. Too late, for them. Kenly smashed into one, thudded in with fists and boots, sent the man gasping and staggering away, Don Rodrigo flung himself upon the other, long clubbed pistol at work. He could fight, this Spaniard.

"To the boat, Conchita—all of you!" lifted his voice. "I follow. Quickly!"

"With me, Don Hugo!" and she was at Kenly's side, grasping his arm, knife in her hand glimmering dully under the bracketed street light.

They ran, dodging among curses and scrambling forms, shouts lifting to them from farther along the street. The fog had thinned out spottily here. They scurried from cover to cover, not knowing what might be in the ambush or the open ahead. The girl was nimble. She ran lightly, swiftly, needing Kenly's arm less than he had need of her guidance.

Pablo and Matilde fell to their rear, thudding and pattering along. And further in the rear lifted the hard, savage American shouts, dully echoing. Other shouts made reply ahead. The alarm had spread. With quick swerve, the girl shunted the chase into another lane, and here the crooked trail was one of darkness, obscurity. She must have the senses of a cat, thought Kenly.

Now she slackened pace. There were twists and corners, sudden turnings, wild bawdy voices bursting from tavern and inn where lights tokened cross streets. But the revelers were snug under roof, and the lights shone dimly; the fog, down here along the river, was thick again and dense. These, Kenly could guess, were not the precincts of the Hotel Beausejour.

Yet the smells of the wharves and the river-miasma hung in the air. Suddenly they broke out upon the levee street, merging with the fog and the night; the dank breath of the river, flowing darkly below them and lapping the pilings of the plank landings, was chill to the face. The girl guided surely, mounting to the levee and sensing all obstruction.

The tethered crafts lay ghostly and silent.

Her figure halted at a gang-plank, signaled by a dim light at the inboard end.

"Your hand, Don Hugo! We are here." Then her voice pierced ahead, urgent yet guarded. "*Alerta! Alerta!* Santa Anna!"

Dim ghostly forms stirred upon the boat, already warned by Pablo. Kenly piloted her down the incline of the narrow bridge and they halted, panting. She was speaking rapidly to the dim figures around, giving orders. After a moment, Pablo and the old dame hove into sight, scrambling along with curses and wheezy breaths. Then the clatter of boot heels on wood, and Captain Estremadura bore in and briskly drove at them with his voice. Finding all here, he snapped orders.

"In with the plank! Cast loose a little and float free—quickly, there. What a cursed fog! But it welcomes us, it enfolds us."

The boat swung to slacked hawsers, lines were hauled in, vague curses and oaths slobbered down along the bulwarks as men worked. A small schooner, as Kenly now became aware. He laughed softly, as he could still hear the bayings of pursuit, muffled by distance, sounding at random. Let them hunt him now! No returning for him; the way back was closed by destiny. Mexico it had to be, whether or no.

Ghostly, silent, the wharves and levee melted away, floated into obscurity and mist. Lights flickered and grew. At the girl's voice Kenly descended a companionway and welcome radiance beckoned him on into the cabin.

Damp and musty here. A large lamp swung in gimbals over the center table. Berths on either side, garments hung up, racks at one end, divided by the door. At the other, oddly enough, was a brick-rimmed hearth with a grated brazier. A fireplace on a ship—Kenly laughed at this. A dark, bronzed man with gold rings in his ears was kneeling before this brazier, rousing it to a glow with working bellows, so that fierce little flames began to surge up among the chunks of black coal, and whiffs of sulphurous charcoal rose pungent on the cabin.

The girl swung a chair from the table toward the hearth, and took seat, huddling in her cloak and extending her feet to the blaze. Now, in the light, the silk lining of her dark cloak showed a smear of blood, but she heeded it not. The yellow flames were gaining. The dark man stood up and rested his bellows.

"Float with the tide," said Don Rodrigo. "As soon as we have a breeze, lift sail. Watch with sweeps."

"Mad navigation for river nights," spoke out Kenly, frowning. "That's my business. I tell you—"

THE OTHER swept him a keen look. "Needs must when the devil drives, *señor*. Would you stay tied up to the bank, then?"

Kenly nodded comprehension. The dark man spoke, smilingly, urbane.

"There is little danger, *señores*. Already we can see stars; the fog is lifting out here on the water."

"Have men come?" asked Don Rodrigo.

"Three, *señor*. Others came and went again, for liquor or whatnot. Three remained. They are below, in the extra cabins."

"Very well. There is nothing more. Take charge above."

The man went out, closing the door behind him. Don Rodrigo threw off his cloak and hat and stood with his back to the fire, hands hooked in his pistol-belt. His gaze dwelt upon Kenly. A new authority was in his bearing, a curt crispness in his tone.

"I have decided, *amigo*, that once in Bejar it will be best for you to enlist; as an officer, of course. The Mexican uniform will protect you from the past. There we may find Americans, friends and relatives of our Santiago Bowie; and, you know, word flies like the arrow. Besides, he has many friends in Bejar of Mexican blood. It is now a feud, you comprehend; a life for a life."

"I'm not worried over that," and Kenly smiled grimly.

"But I am," said Don Rodrigo. "What I propose is merely for your own interest. I shall report of you to General Cos, and at first opportunity—well, you have already done Mexico a service. There is nothing you may not expect. Meantime, you will receive a dollar and a quarter per diem; Mexico is generous with her soldiers. As an officer, you may receive more. As for tonight, and the few nights to come," and Don Rodrigo spread his hands helplessly, "you see that these quarters are rather limited. What to do? We must make the best of things. Pablo will show you where you may sleep in all comfort, the best we can arrange. Good night, *señor*."

Doña Maria had tossed away her cloak now, holding her hands out to the brazier. Her hair gleamed with the warm gold of promise, and her flashing smile.

"Until tomorrow, *señor*; go with God!" she said.

There was but one reply to these finalities. Kenly left her to the snug cabin and to her cousin Captain Rodrigo Estremadura. He left her, not without an ugly twist to his thoughts, a quick hot glance at the good captain; but Don Rodrigo was musingly twirling his black mustache, black eyes adrift.

Kenly found the deck listless, lit by lanterns, men at work here and there in slovenly fashion. The fog showed signs of breaking, and a breeze was stirring it into slow whirls. Kenly walked forward, and near a lantern a figure turned to welcome him. A bluff, slatternly fellow, hat pulled down over whiskered face.

"One of us, mister? Viva Santy Anny and hooray for good pickin's!" came the thick, hoarse voice. "I seen you come aboard with that purty baggage. Me, I was a step ahead of you. A fetching dodge, wan't it? A word in a feller's ear, a little tour up the hall to a tidy room, a *señorita* all eyes and smiles to make a man forget his gal! Plenty more like her for the having in Mexico, says she, taking 'era light or dark. Cripes! If it hadn't been for that rumpus—but what's your handle, mister?"

"Kenly's the name."

"I'm Matt Devore. Glad to get acquainted, comrade. Sojer, ain't you? If it hadn't been for that rumpus, the gal would ha' bagged a full company. Hey, did ye know that somebody done for Jim Bowie? Yes, sir." Devore peered more closely at Kenly's profile, his breath sodden with liquor fumes. "By the token, I'm damned if you ain't the feller yourself! You—"

The sharp exclamation broke from him, broke off sharp. Awe was in his voice, incredulity, accusation.

"Be damned to you then, and sheer off," said Kenly. "You're drunk. Take yourself off or I'll handle you, my friend."

"Aye?"

Devore laughed an ugly laugh, and planted defiant legs, "I'm not so swizzled, mister; damn me, will you? Happens—wan't born in the woods to be scared by no owl. Not me. It's all right, now. I see you setting in the Beausejour, and you wasn't there when next I looked in. The place was in a gabble and the search on for somebody special. I cut stick for the levee, and next I see, you're leading the *señorita* down the plank.

"Ho, you're the feller, all right, I know your mug! But it's hoss and hoss, comrade. You're for t'other side the fence and you've got good reason, including the gal no doubt. So am I. Now look'ee, comrade! Done for Jim Bowie, and your name's up from Tennessee to Nachitoches, ain't it? Well, me the same.

I've quit the bloody army, and it's me to drill dragoons. Sergeant major, and a dollar and a quarter a day or more, and stripes down the legs instead of down the back."

THE MAN'S assumption of enforced friendliness, of criminal association, angered Kenly. The fog was into him again, the musty night; the thing most of all burning in his mind was thought of the cabin below. Cousins, indeed!

"I don't care who the devil you are or what you've been," he snapped. "Make yourself scarce or you'll be hanging on a sawyer you won't like."

"Riverman, huh?" Devore sneered, and spat thickly over the rail. "Been in the pilot house, huh? Don't you try to come the officer over Matt Devore; it's no go. You ain't in the cabin now, nor me either, and we're all in the same boat. We'll be sojering for Santy Anny, and ye needn't take no brag about doing for Jim Bowie, neither. You're a better man than him, and there's better'n you."

Kenly turned to the rail, getting a grip on himself, and held silence.

"It happens I'm in a snarl. If I get in another, or Texas gets the gouge holt on Santy Anny," growled on the man, "and if a swap of sides looks convenient for one or t'other of us, or both, you play fair! Understand? You play fair and keep mum, and the same goes for me. Happen we go over to the Texans, you may get the stripes and the drumhead for me, but it'll be the rope or a slit gizzard for you. Them Bowie boys are screamers, and they ain't the only fellers to use a knife, neither. Mind me."

With this, Devore swaggered away and was swallowed up. Kenly leaned over the rail, a little sick at heart over the whole thing. Then he was aware of another figure, of a friendly voice. The second time that this same voice had reached into his sick soul.

"It is Pablo, *señor*, Pablo Saccaplata, and I have prepared a bed for the *señor*, on the ropes and canvas down the other hatch. The *señor* will be more comfortable than among those men

forward; they are not of his kind. Ah, *señor*," and for an instant
Pablo hesitated, then plunged on. "I am an honest man. They
would have left me; I heard the words but my legs would not
work. You saved my life, and my life is yours, *señor*. You will
pardon, but—"

Again the man hesitated. Kenly had swung around.

"Well, what is it? Go ahead; I'll repeat nothing. Something
you want to tell me?"

"But yes." Pablo dropped his voice. "It is Doña Maria, *señor*.
In Bejar you will find her no *doña*, no fine lady, but known as
Conchita la Blonda. She is good to look upon, *señor*, as far as
the eye may see; but in Bejar the *señor* may learn much—"

Pablo hesitated again. Kenly smiled grimly.

"Go ahead, *hombre*. I'm getting in debt to you, if I mistake
not. Go on."

"*Diablo!* Well, Don Rodrigo may do what he has doubtless
promised to do, but one does not expect meat from the wolf.
The *señor* is going to be enlisted? Better so. I, too, am of the
ranks of Mexico, a soldier. We shall be fellow soldiers, perhaps.
I will tell my mother and step-sister about you, *señor*. She is a
good girl, *señor*, that step-sister of mine, and she has all the
brains that I, Pablo Saccaplata, lack so sadly. Now, if the *señor*
wishes to go to bed, I will lead him. The *señor* is not angry?"

Kenly, for answer, put his arm about the wide shoulders, his
fingers pressed the serape; he felt a quick, unaccustomed burst
of affection for this fellow of honesty and blunt words. Somehow
he sensed true friendship here, a rare thing, unwonted loyalty
in the pocked visage.

CHAPTER IV

DARK ATTACK

THE SQUALID fishing-village of San Blas sprawled in a glamor shamelessly borrowed from the morning sunlight. This white blaze of radiance softened the sandy shores and sparkling blue of the long, land-locked Matagorda Bay of southern Texas. Palmettos broke the level lines of shore and sky.

The schooner, skimming down the broadening Mississippi, without event had gone swinging on long reaches across the white-tossing Gulf. During the traverse Kenly had seen little of the *doña*, who had kept to her cabin; had seen no more than the little of the *señor capitan*, who shared the cabin with her; had exchanged few words with Devore and two companions of like stamp. To put it bluntly, he had been seasick. Still, he fared well enough, with sleeping quarters to himself. His meals, such as they were, the solicitous Pablo fetched him.

Obviously, the cabin was to be regarded as inviolate. His first surprise and even shock at the situation passed into a shrug; then he laughed at himself, at the whole thing.

It was only in this last hour, when the palmettos and pines of the low shores were growing larger in the view, that Pablo bore him the invitation: "Doña Maria and the *capitan* would be pleased to have the *señor* join them."

So Kenly left the midships rail and went aft to the stern. A homeless man, he had been feeling a bit lonely; the slanted glance and the flitter of a smile from the girl heartened him like a lighted window for a wayfarer. Whatever her actions might imply, he was content to read her with his eyes and accept what good they saw.

Don Rodrigo turned to him with words of courtesy.

"Welcome to Mexico, *señor*. Our apologies for what might seem neglect; but Doña Maria is a poor sailor, and I am worse. Ah, what a sickness it is, this of the accursed sea! We haven't stirred from the cabin the whole time. Thank heaven, we'll soon be where our legs are of use. We land yonder; it is only a few days to San Antonio de Bejar—or, in the common parlance, Bejar."

To an American ear the word sounded exactly like "bear," the soft guttural being almost unheard; had it not been for his conversation with Crockett, indeed, Kenly might have thought the name of the town to be "Bear." In the Spanish, an accent makes all the difference.

"Surely Don Hugo will forgive us," lisped Doña Maria, with an arch look of mock sadness. "Has not he himself, perhaps, been ill also?"

"*Viva Dios!*" cackled old Matilde. "I smell the blessed land; indeed, I vowed a candle or so—but what matter? It is well known that when danger is past, God is always forgotten."

There was pleasant talk, and Kenly warmed toward the girl he had been cursing for a slut and a decoy. Seasickness? It might well be true, and the thought banished the rankling suspicion, or rather lessened it.

The schooner slid through the narrow channel of the long sand-reef that framed the bay, and anchored off the village. By swaying ladder and fishermen's ready boats, transfer from ship to shore was accomplished. "*Viva Dios!*" again, from many a throat, and Kenly grunted with relief at the feel of the dry sand. A riverman was not a seaman by a good deal.

The worthy Don Rodrigo was a man of foresight; a man, evidently, of far influence. Mules and horses were in readiness here, as though stationed to await his coming. Doña Maria mounted side-saddle. Matilde, with vows renewed for journey's end, was packed into a pannier balanced by baggage. Now they were a party of eight who set forth. Don Rodrigo, Kenly, Pablo armed with a flintlock musket, bell-mouthed on the blunder-buss order, the two women, Devore and his two companions.

Don Rodrigo brooked no delay.

"This is no good place for us," he said truly. "We shall reach Goliad tonight. It is garrisoned; we shall rest in comfort. Bejar is then within three days, for any like us who travel light and fast."

He spurred forth. Doña Maria fell back to rein in beside Kenly. Matilde and the others trailed along, with Pablo and his bell-mouth closing the rear. Don Rodrigo twisted his mustache and pointed.

"You see, the road is well made for us!"

A broad trail, evidently trampled down very recently, led straight to the northwest. The liquid eyes of Doña Maria sparkled as they followed it across the low, hillocky prairie, and a gay laugh broke from her lips.

"Reinforcements for Bejar came this way—*viva!* Once in Bejar we shall be safe. And tonight we shall reach the old pre-sidio of La Bahia; Goliad, they call it nowadays. The second fortress in Texas, my Hugo! Bejar is the first. Well, we shall find Colonel Sandoval at Goliad. He is a true *caballero*, a conquis-tador—"

Perchance finding Kenly's eye a trifle inattentive to her chatter, she came stirrup to stirrup with him, so that her foot touched against his leg and struck him out of his reverie. Her smile was witching.

"Ah, my friend, you are not angry with Conchita? How I longed for one word from you, for a touch of your hand, during those days of savage sickness! But with so many other men about, it was impossible. The saints forbid! There would have been talk. Yet I was so miserable, my *caballero*—"

No, Kenly was not angry, and he found words to say as much,

Don Rodrigo's pistol belched smoke.

though at the back of his head he found himself laughing at the effrontery of her excuses. What he said, he scarcely knew. That confounded golden haze limited his horizons. Conchita indeed! The very nickname might have told him enough, yet he rode on, foolish with the present moment, compassed about by a girl with a sly alluring smile, a purling voice.

THUS A mile or two, no more, of the march. Then the girl's face changed, hardened, as her gaze swept out. A word broke from Don Rodrigo in front; she echoed it under her breath. The men behind echoed it.

"*Tejanos! Tejanos!*"

A squad of half a dozen riders were cantering in upon the trail ahead. They dipped below a rise, surmounted it, and then spread out into a ragged front as they drew challenging rein across the trail. Their leader came to meet the party, one hand lifted in signal of parley and peace.

"*Buenos dias* to you, gentlemen and ladies!" He was of erect, shapely figure, a man of perhaps twenty-five, of sharp face, hazel eyes, reddish stubble showing brightly against a skin that did not tan. He had an unsmiling mouth, and revealed light sandy hair when he swept off his wide wool hat. Closely fitting gray shirt, belted trousers tucked into high boots, sheathed knife and holstered pistol. His address had been in form, but careless, cool, somewhat cavalier. His thoughtful eyes ran over the party and settled upon Don Rodrigo, who made him answer.

"The same to you, *señor*. And what is your pleasure?"

"A word with you. My name is Travis. William Barrett Travis."

"And well known," said Don Rodrigo, a trifle grimly. "But not favorably known to Mexico, *señor*. I believe that your arrest has been ordered as a rebel."

The Texans grinned at this response, whose frankness pleased them. Travis shrugged. His hazel eyes glinted with a certain mirthless satisfaction. He was not a man of gay humor; his manner held an earnestness, a disturbing intentness.

"Possibly. I am one of those damned Texans who are bent upon getting Texas her rights as a state. You're heading for Bejar?"

"If so, why not?" demanded Don Rodrigo coolly.

"No objections," Travis said, again carelessly. "But don't figure on a long stay. We let General Cos and his column pass through. You might tell him in the name of Texas that we'll call on him later. I see you have Americans with you." He glanced at Kenly and the others, and broke into English: "Are you men for Bejar going along with this Mexican outfit?"

Devore had ridden up.

"What's it to you if we are?" he demanded aggressively. "This is Mexico, ain't it? A free trail and good company if it suits us."

"Yes? Just take care you're not found on the wrong side when the time comes," and Travis regarded him coldly, appraisingly. "If you men are Americans, there's only one place for you; that's with Texas. Hell, would you go for Mexico when a free Texas is in the running?"

"Every man for himself is my motto," Devore growled.

"Where I'm going or what I'm thinking to do is my own business, mister."

"I reckon you're the kind that has no choice in some matters," said Travis, and his cold stare looked Devore down. He turned his attention to Kenly. "You're a different stamp, I see. I can't object to your trail partner, sir; she's any man's reason for riding to paradise or the devil, but—but—"

He started slightly, and his voice died. His eyes suddenly focused upon Kenly's person; Kenly was as suddenly aware that his coat had swung open in the breeze. It was the knife, whose haft protruded from a crude leather sheath hastily stitched together aboard the schooner, and now looped to his belt.

"I'd admire to know, sir," and Travis lapsed into the easy drawl of his native Carolina, "how you traded Jim Bowie out of his knife."

A cold hand clutched at Kenly's heart. Then he managed to iron out the stammer of his tongue, and forced a thin smile.

"This knife? It was presented to me, sir. You may be mistaken in it."

"Not I; that handle I'd know among a thousand," said Travis coldly. "Special made, handle and blade, and I don't reckon Jim Bowie was likely to give his choice knife away, without you're a special friend of his. Your secret, maybe his, since you're not inclined to talk. When I see him again, I'll ask him who outtraded him, and tell him where I saw that knife of his. I'm not likely to forget your face. Your servant, madame. *Adios*, all."

TRAVIS REINED his horse aside, and the Texans separated to let the travelers pass. Kenly caught a half mocking word from one of them: "Hope you sleep well in Goliad, you *hombres!*" but he thought little of this until later.

He did think considerably upon William Barrett Travis, and inwardly cursed the whole episode of the knife. Jim Bowie seem to be tailing him clear into Mexico; that was to be expected of such a man, alive or dead. This meeting, the clean-cut ominous words of Travis, the business of the knife, all left Kenly moody and dark, so that even the gay chatter of the lovely Doña Maria failed to inspirit him.

The sun crossed the zenith, and there was brief halt for rest and luncheon. The sun dropped steadily into the west, and they quickened their pace. With twilight they were riding a trail of beaten gold, but Don Rodrigo was cursing their slowness, for this was the rainy season, and with night all these lowlands would be hazy with fog.

No fog tonight, however. The moon in its first quarter succeeded to the twilight, and the moon itself was dropping from sight when, at this, the end of the long march, the feeble lights of the old presidio of La Bahia, now the military post and town of Goliad, twinkled through the darkness.

This place, founded in 1722, like many others in Texas bore more than one name, due to the ancient custom of secular authority being separate from the mission establishment. Bejar itself had been San Antonio de Valero, San Fernando de Bejar, and other such names.

Challenge of sentries, gates acreak in the fading moonlight, a glimpse of walls and uniforms as lanterns bobbed; this was all Kenly saw of old Goliad on the San Antonio river. Unaccustomed to riding, he was stiff and sore and weary. Don Rodrigo and the two women disappeared into headquarters. Kenly and the rest were served with food and given lodging in an adobe attached to the presidio buildings.

"Hope you sleep well in Goliad, you *hombres!*" The jibing, sinister words came back into Kenly's mind as he sank away, engulfed by the snores and gurgles of his companions. Then all was forgotten.

Suddenly he wakened, with upward lunge like that of a diver blindly bursting into the air again. He found himself on his feet, ears ringing, senses wide awake. A gunshot had burst close by. Now came another, with a wild tumult of yells, hails and replies, shouted orders, the scuff-scuff of running feet, and more shouts.

Devore and his fellows were up.

"An attack!" yelled Devore. "We're trapped here—make a slope for it!"

Running feet paused at their door, and it was banged open as a man entered. The wild clamor outside was redoubled; then, with inward rush of fresh night air, came the quick announcement of Pablo.

"With me, *señores!* The Texans are taking the town—come swiftly!"

They stumbled out, jostling each other. Kenly caught Pablo's arm.

"The women?"

"Safe, *señor*; they will come. Horses are waiting."

Everything was dark, strange, confusing. The tumult of fighting increased; gunfire, yells and shouts, the reiterant splintering of planks under axes. But ahead, where quiet still ruled the night, horses and mules were being saddled. The voice of Don Rodrigo leaped forth.

"*Valgame!* No time to lose; all here? Get aboard and off, then. The place is taken. To me, Pablo! In the lead."

There was mounting and riding, the gasping plaints of old Matilde stabbing the darkness. Don Rodrigo was keeping his whole party intact, Kenly observed, and the devil take anyone else!

Out of the hapless town now. A cannon exploded somewhere behind, then another. The fight died away upon the night, and Kenly was aware of Doña Maria once more at his side, her silvery laugh ringing out. Now, when he could not see her glamorous eyes and face, he began to be a little afraid of this lovely creature. As though something intangible reached forth and touched him, waking a queer revulsion in his heart, making him recoil from what he knew not. Then he laughed the feeling away.

"So, *Hugo, mio*—what a night!" said she, gaily enough. "They are the rebels; but our good Rodrigo was ready. He had prepared everything. And Colonel Sandoval had been warned of an attack."

"Who is it? That man Travis?"

"God knows. Are names exchanged in a night assault?" She laughed again. "And what lies ahead of us is hard to say. The settlements are safe, but the wide chaparral holds Tejanos, raiding Comanches, outlaws, plunderers. To ride this road without a cavalry escort is sheer madness—no time for escort now, though. A wild place, this state of Texas for which you are come to fight!"

KENLY SAID nothing. He was getting no great joy of his company; but the thought of that knife under his belt, of the dead face of Jim Bowie, held him fast bound.

Presently Don Rodrigo slackened the pace from flight to common sense, and they rode on under the paling stars. Here was no beaten trail of reinforcements marching for Bejar, but a rough prairie route taken at venture. It would not be long now to morning.

With graying sky, they halted. Somewhere behind them rose a mad drumming of hoofbeats; Pablo shouted, and a voice made response. A rider came up with them, a private soldier sticking somehow in the saddle of a dragoon horse, white with foam, staggering with exhaustion.

"What killing, what blood!" he babbled in hysteric panic. "The town is taken, the fortress taken. Those Tejanos are not men but devils! The garrison scattered, captured, dead! All the towns on the gulf coast, Anahuac and the rest, are being taken."

The party halted here. Kenly approached Doña Maria. With brief, delicious surrender of her soft form, she yielded to his arms for a moment as she slid to the ground. The groans of old Matilde brought laughter. They all made bivouac; Pablo struck fire, to warm hands and feet, and in the chill dawn they huddled about the blaze.

Coyotes sang mournful pæan to the departing stars. The sun flashed through the reddened sky at last. A stream was close by. There was breakfast, of a sort, before they mounted and rode on. All about was untrodden prairie. The course lay northwest, and San Antonio de Bejar could not be missed. Assuredly a wide, far land, this state of Texas, to lie under whichever hand was stronger, white or brown.

The morning passed, and again it was the noon rest. No other fugitives joined them. Again the onward stint into afternoon. Ever the endless horizon, trees and grassy slopes, unbroken by human touch. Well watered was this country. Suddenly Kenly was startled out of his moody reflections. A wild, explosive cry burst from Doña Maria.

"*Santo Dios*—look! Look!"

All heads turned. Clustered moving dots were sweeping in along the trail; a company of riders. Pursuit? And for what? Kenly felt the knife stir against his thigh as though nudging him: Here comes vengeance for the dead! But Pablo's were the keenest eyes of all. A sharp bleat escaped him.

"*Los Indios!* They are *los Indios, capitan!* Now we are all dead people."

"That is so, *amigo*." Don Rodrigo was prompt, soldierly, cool. "We are not dead yet, however. Gain that knoll ahead. You, Pablo, to the rear with your musket; you," to the fugitive private, "join him. The rest, keep with me." He lifted his mount, with an oath. "Make for that knoll above the stream. There are more of the devils. This land is accursed!"

Another party had appeared, off to the right. Now the horses spurted right willingly, but the knoll was cruelly distant.

Kenly's eye was caught by the girl. Her golden hair had loosened in the breeze, in the shock of gallop; her color was high, her eyes were bright, she rode fearless, a devil of laughter touching her lips. Above the dull pounding of hooves and the gusty panting of the animals, rose the lamentations of old Matilde.

With gleeful yelps, with heels hammering, quirts at work, lances tossing, the Indians upon the flank bore in rapidly. *Los*

Comanchos! The dread word was tossed from mouth to mouth. The Comanches! So close were the Indians that the paint was plain upon their grinning visages and swart bodies. Kenly saw the flash of a knife in the girl's hand, saw her lips curl in a snarl that hardened her face until he scarce knew it.

"They've got us. Make the best of it!"

Don Rodrigo's voice rose coolly. He rode with rein free, a pistol in either hand. The angle of chase and pursuit narrowed rapidly; in the rear, the clamor of the first group of Indians sounded louder. In all the wide prairie, the horizon came down to this; quarry and pack, curses and vows, yells and supplications amid the thundering hoofbeats, and the knoll that rose from the stream.

The angle closed. The Comanches split; one squad hammered to the fore, to cut off pursuit, the other squad raced parallel with the whites. At short range, Don Rodrigo's right-hand pistol belched smoke. The horse of the leading Indian lurched and went down, kicking, the rider pinioned beneath it. The other Comanches swerved aside. Arrows glittered and hissed in air.

AN OATH burst from Don Rodrigo; a shaft jutted out from his shoulder; Doña Maria uttered a frantic cry; her horse had stumbled, was down. Kenly reined about; ah she was still seated, her horse was struggling up! Then came shock of collision as red and white came together. Kenly bared his knife and hurled himself headlong into the wild mêlée of tossing manes and striking arms.

Sharp it was and swift. Devore and his two fellows were lashing out with fists and feet, old Matilde was clawing, Pablo was unhorsed but fighting with clubbed musket. At the bridle of Doña Maria was an Indian, another reaching brown arm for her, as her little knife flashed vainly. The fugitive private had fled the Goliad strife in vain, for a lance went through his throat and he died with blood bubbling on his lips.

Kenly's knife freed the girl's horse from its captor, sheared through side and heart; the death-yell stabbed out, and in stabbed a lance-point, slitting Kenly's shirt and searing under his arm. Then he was at grips with the Indian who had clutched the girl, and who clutched him now in desperation, seizing his knife-wrist, glaring into his face. Then the wild eyes grew wider, fastened upon the knife that trembled between them. A shrill, high yell broke from the Indian. He loosened his grip, flung himself away, sent his horse about, rearing. To his yells, the others drew off. The girl's horse sprang forward anew. As by a miracle the struggle was over and they were in flight again.

Thus they made sanctuary and gained the knoll with its trees. Back upon the prairie the groups of Comanches had come together and were milling amid a rise of voices. Here upon the bushy rise, the wounded Don Rodrigo painfully swung from the saddle.

"Here we stay; off, everybody! Our one chance is to hold them from here. So our fugitive is done for, eh? Anyone else hurt?"

"You, Rodrigo," cried out the girl. "That arrow—*Dios mio!* And Don Hugo has a lance thrust. Look at the blood on his shirt!"

"The arrow announces itself, fair cousin," said Don Rodrigo grimly. "Here with a knife, somebody! No time to lose."

"That's work for me, little general." Matilde wheezed forward. "I've done the same many a time ere this. Yes, indeed! Ah, what doings! If flesh and blood can stand a ride like this, I'll live to a hundred. Come, come, let's see your skin! It's no time for modesty, *capitan*. Besides, I'm an old woman."

Kenly stared as he listened. No shrieks, no hysterics—why, there was iron in these Mexican women, and no mistake! The don bared his shoulder and arm. Matilde eyed the hurt, wiped at the blood, fingered the shaft.

"*Chut!* I can feel the point. All we need is a sharp knife. Your *cuchillo grande*, Mister American! It's cut more than cheese already, I can see."

Kenly handed over the knife, still dripping red. The arrow had lodged in Don Rodrigo's shoulder; deflected by the bone, it had penetrated almost through the upper arm. Matilde slashed, and the steel grated on the arrow-head. She slashed at the feathered end, while Don Rodrigo cursed heartily, until the shaft was severed. Then she shoved the point, and what remained of the shaft, through the wound.

"Devil take you!" grunted Don Rodrigo, his eyes sweeping toward the Indians.

"May the devil be deaf," and Matilde grinned. "The devil gave it; you might not be so good a bargain next time. I'll dress the wound with cold water in a minute. Here, *caballero!*" and she turned to Kenly. "Let's see your touch of the cold steel!"

"It's nothing," and Kenly smiled. "The bleeding's stopped already, the skin's no more than broken. Leave it alone. What's the program, Don Rodrigo?"

"Wait, camp, rest, be comfortable," said the other promptly, but grimly enough. "They'll hesitate to attack this knoll; if we were on the prairie, they'd ride us down in a moment. A fire may gain us help. We're not far from the Bejar road. We can spend the night here, for they'll not attack at night. Pablo!"

"Yes, my captain."

"Water the horses; Don Hugo will take the musket, to cover you. Bring the canteens full from the creek. The Indians are talking; we must get water while we have the chance. One of them, one of us, dead; life for life."

"Your knife, *señor,*" and Matilde handed the steel to Kenly, who wiped it on his thigh and sheathed it. Then he joined Pablo, collecting the horses, taking them down to the creek. Devore and his two companions, little hurt, sulked at one side.

"That old woman has a devil in her," Pablo said admiringly. "However, *señor,* I am sure we shall all get safe to Bejar."

"How so?" demanded Kenly, keeping an eye on the Indians.

"I have two there who are praying for me," Pablo responded. "They are my mother and Josefa, my half-sister. They are both good women."

CHAPTER V

MATT DEVORE'S PROPOSITION

THE COMANCHES clustered in talk, unheeding the horses at the stream. Then one of them came forward afoot, unarmed, arm extended in the peace sign. He was a waddling, burly figure; and Kenly recognized his late antagonist. The Indian halted mid-way, fearlessly enough. Don Rodrigo rose to his feet, but Pablo intervened.

"Let the captain not show his wound. I will go down, if I have a knife—"

Kenly handed over the blade. Pablo stowed it away, then descended to talk with the Indian. For some little time he and the Comanche spoke together; then Pablo came back up the knoll. With a shrug he returned the knife to Kenly.

"He is a chief, but only a little one," he reported. "And he respected the knife much, and admires it. So we go on. He says that if we give him Doña Maria we may go on in peace. The young woman with shining hair—"

The girl cried out indignantly. Don Rodrigo smiled and shrugged.

"Bah! You told him no?"

"Not necessary," said Pablo. "He says they will wait. By morning, his *capitan grande*, his head chief, will be here; they await him. It was through fear that the lady might be harmed, that they drew back. We'll have to surrender the lady in the morning, for the head chief is El Lobo Rojo and—"

Old Matilde came to her feet with a wild squeal.

"What's that? Red Wolf, you say? Praise God a thousand times! Yes, we shall wait, we shall see; now all is well!"

"What the devil!" exclaimed Don Rodrigo, staring at her. "Are you mad?"

The old crone cackled excitedly. "Rest easy, little general! Remember, I gave this American a knife of value, and to you I gave the San Saba treasure map; and I may yet give us all our lives! When one door closes, another opens. We shall see in the morning, so have patience. One cannot hasten the dawn by rising early, so permit me to sit with what I know."

"You talk like a fool," snapped Don Rodrigo angrily.

"To the blind, all cats are black, little general," and Matilde crouched down, chuckling to herself and hugging her knees, while she mumbled like a witch.

The Comanches kept the truce, and the day drew to a close. The sun couched under a canopy of twink, the twilight lessened, the stars flocked into the wake of the westering moon. The last of their food was shared, and Kenly, awaiting his time to go on watch, stretched out under one of the pine trees and fell asleep. His mood was miserable.

He was under no illusion in regard to his companions. Step by step, he had gone down the scale since that steamboat explosion. With each step, he had played in worse luck; and he was assured that his evil destiny was yet far from played out.

Suddenly he wakened and clutched at his knife. A stealthy rustle amid the brush—the thought of Comanches rushed upon him. Then a low voice growled.

"It's me, Matt Devore. Awake, huh?"

Kenly sat up. "What d'you want?"

"Confab." The other squatted beside him. "None of us boys like this mess. With them Texans nabbing Goliad and damn near nabbing us, and these Injuns to boot, the whole business is like that game where the jack takes the ace. We vote to play what hand we have and streak out, and Bejar be blowed. What d'you say?"

"I don't get you," murmured Kenly.

"Give the gal to the Injuns, take the guns, and leave them two Mexicans and the old hag to bargain themselves off. Four of us ag'in one and a half. That pelado with the musket can be easy handled. Two pistols, a gun, your knife and a clear trail. The Injuns will be tickled pink to let us go."

"Well?" asked Kenly. "After that, what?"

"Not Goliad, you bet; that's closed to us, and worse than closed to you, after what that feller Travis said," and Devore chuckled softly. "Not Bejar, and not back to New Orleans. I don't want no U. S. marshal grabbing me. Where, d'you say? Why, for them San Saba mines of Jim Bowie's, you bet!"

"The San Saba mines! What the devil do you know about 'em?"

"YOU MIGHT'S well ask how I know the Injuns want the gal. I'm no fool," and Devore laughed. "You got Jim Bowie's knife, and I know how you got it. Prob'ly you got his map of the silver mines at the same time. I heard cabin talk on that schooner. The old dame wasn't hushed; you might's well try to clap a stopper on a cannon. I know enough Spanish to tell a few things. Either you or the don has the map. It's for us to take it and light out with the hosses for them mines. Then, by cripes, there'll be gals a-plenty and we can make terms with Jim Bowie."

Kenly started. "Bowie's dead."

"Yeah; we'll make terms with him in hell. What d'you say to it?"

"I say you're a damned scoundrel," snapped Kenly. "I've heard enough from you. Get to hell out of here and don't try any tricks. I'll be watching you."

Devore caught his breath angrily, then growled an oath.

"So that's it, huh? All right. And I'll be watchin' you, mister. I know what you know, and maybe a bit more. I mean to have a go for them Almagres mines, and don't you forget it, you cussed aristocrat!"

Devore went rustling away. Unable to sleep again, Kenly presently rose and sought out the others about the embers of the fire. The figure of Don Rodrigo half rose.

"*Que cosa?* What's the matter?"

"It's Kenly. Just looking around a bit."

"*Alerta!* That's good. I can't sleep with this cursed shoulder. Did I hear talking?"

"Your recruits are uneasy."

Kenly sat down. Doña Maria, covered with her cloak, was breathing regularly. Old Matilde, beside her, gurgled and sniffled. Don Rodrigo laughed softly.

"Uneasy? Naturally; but we are in the hand of God. Why that old woman prates about El Lobo Rojo, I don't know. You bear yourself well, *señor*. I shall remember," and his pistols clattered slightly as he drew his cloak further over himself.

"I can take the watch, if you like," said Kenly.

"Not necessary, *señor*. I'm on the alert," came the voice of Pablo.

By this, and by the readiness of Don Rodrigo, Kenly suspected that it was all over with Devore's proposition. He left the sleepers and made his way to where Pablo was located, on the crest of the rise, musket close to hand.

"How goes it?"

"Well enough, *señor*. The Indians will not attack; we have only the others to worry about."

"Eh? What others?"

"The three Americans. They talk among themselves too much; what is well said is quickly said, eh? But they are like guests and fish; always the time comes when they begin to stink. I sit here, God sends tomorrow, and we'll be out of this."

"Eh? You wouldn't give the *señorita* to the Indians?"

"Never fear; Matilde will attend to it. That old she-devil holds half of hell in her past life. Listen—she sounds as though she had a frog in her nose! Go back to sleep, *señor*. You did not save my life for nothing; in Bejar you will always have a friend."

Kenly dozed off, fitfully. The dawn brightened, and the camp stirred. Old Matilde scuffled around. Doña Maria sat up, somewhat wan and pinched, to luxuriate like a cat in the first warm beams of the sun. Kenly felt her ready smile and glance; she freely adjusted her hair, so that her lifted arms framed her in a glow of beauty. Don Rodrigo cursed the stiffness of his wound. Devore and the other two sidled in, frowzy and lowering. The horses were watered.

The Comanches, down below, stirred and moved. A single figure advanced on foot toward the base of the knoll; not the figure of the previous day, but another in every aspect. An Indian, equipped in form and presence to claim the eye. They stared at him.

Straight and lithe, skin shimmering like that of a new-cast snake, agleam with paint and barbaric ornaments, twin long braids transfixed at the scalp with a bobbing feather, naked but for moccasins and clout, he strode forward like a young god come for tribute, masterful and aware. There was a ruddiness to him, even to his hair—not black but warmly tinted, coppery, verging upon red. High proud nose, aquiline visage, cruel eyes; all this was the more plain by reason of being so extraordinary, fascinating the onlooker with its exotic touch.

"By thunder, there's a swaggerin' copper-bottom for you!" grunted an American.

"*Dios!* What an Indian!" exclaimed Don Rodrigo in admiration. Doña Maria had risen, her eyes fixed and kindling, a strange, savage eagerness in her face.

"*Viva!* What a man!" she murmured.

"*Viva Dios*, indeed—it is he!" cried old Matilde, earnestly squinting. "Now everything is very simple. I myself will talk with him."

"You think a chief will talk with a woman?" scoffed Don Rodrigo, and laughed.

"Or are you going to offer your charms to ransom us all?"

"PERHAPS," ANSWERED Matilde with some

dignity. "Did he not suck life from these breasts? Was not I, when a younger woman, five years among the Comanches? And a girl of parts might do worse," she added. "Yes, he hung to me late; there was none other for him, and none for me, and I liked the feel of him. His mother was an Apache in the chief's tent. She died in childbirth the same time I lost my baby. And now he is a great chief, and will remember me; I'll speak to him in his own tongue.

"*Dios!* What a credit he is to my milk! I'll talk with him."

"Go along, then," said Don Rodrigo in amazement. Doña Maria turned and spoke.

"I'll go with you, Matilde!"

"Stay here with the devil," snapped the old hag, and scurried out. Don Rodrigo spoke sharply at the girl; she looked at him for a long moment as though she did not see him, then turned again to the scene below, her eyes dilated, eager. One would have thought her bewitched by the sight of that young Indian. And he, as his cruel eyes searched those on the knoll, seemed to fasten his gaze upon her as she poised there, bright of hair, breathlessly intent.

He made a gesture with his hand, as though in greeting.

Then Matilde had come down to him, clucking at him in his own tongue. After a swift exchange of words, remembering that his own warriors were watching, he so far broke down his dignity as to lift her hand to his cheek. Gestures, words, rapid and energetic. Then, while he waited, Matilde turned and hurried back up the slope.

"What is it?" exclaimed the tense Don Rodrigo. "What terms?"

"Patience! I am not a gun," she panted as she came up. "Everything is settled. Doña Maria stays. I told him she is my daughter. So—"

"What?" struck in the girl sharply, almost too sharply. "He doesn't want me?"

"No, my pet. After all, it wouldn't be so bad. If I were

younger—" then she broke off, at the angry look of Don Rodrigo. "He wishes a present, that is all. He has heard of a certain knife, and I promised it to him. Give it up, and he'll go away and we're free. I'm sure Don Hugo will give up the knife," she added half-maliciously. "He wears it well, but the overload is the load that kills. Eh, *señor?*"

Kenly nodded. He was willing enough to be rid of Jim Bowie's knife. He plucked it out and extended it to Don Rodrigo; the silver inlay glinted in the sunlight like the cunning alitted eyes of a basking reptile.

"It's yours, captain."

"God forbid!" and Don Rodrigo laughed. "It's something with short legs and a long tongue. Here, Pablo—toss it out to that brown hidalgo yonder!"

"No, no!" Old Matilde snatched at the knife. "He's not a dog to be thrown a bone! I'll carry it to him."

Doña Maria stopped her abruptly, eyes blazing.

"Fool!" cried the girl angrily. "Fool! We need that man as a friend—oh, what folly! If you had let me go down to him, if you hadn't told him that lie about my being your daughter— why, you've jeopardized everything! If he were a friend, and the mines lying in his country—"

With an angry snarl, Matilde scuttled past her and down the slope. Then the girl ran forward a few steps and halted clear of brush, and threw out her arms. Her voice rang down the level sunlight, her cloak flew back, her bright hair flowed down her slender warm body.

She was a picture of allure, of beauty all aglow.

"*Capitan Grande!* Come to me in Bejar, and come soon. It is a lie that I am her daughter. Come soon, in Bejar!"

The young chief lifted his hand. "In Bejar, Bejar!" he repeated ringingly.

Don Rodrigo burst out in horrified protest that she was risking all their lives, and the girl whirled around upon him angrily.

"Am I taking orders from you?" she broke forth hotly. "Have a care, or you'll go a longer journey than you've just gone! We need that chief in Bejar. We can make use of him. I can get him there. I know my business—"

UNDER HER storm of passion Don Rodrigo subsided. But Kenly, watching, was startled. Was the girl thinking of luring this glorious wild young chief to San Antonio? So she said; but as to her intent—well, that was another matter. Kenly had not missed the play of emotions in her features. His eyes were opened in regard to her. He thought, a little sadly, a little grimly, that he might ever be made a fool of by her; and yet he would be aware of his own folly, at least.

He turned again to the scene below. Red Wolf took the knife from Matilde, with scarcely a glance at it. From his wrist he wrenched a broad silver bracelet and his voice lifted, as his hand made the peace sign.

"*Plata del almagre*, silver of the red earth, for the *señorita!*"

The girl heard and turned. She raised her arm, returning the sign; the breeze fluttered her dress.

Her eyes widened and a laugh touched her lips.

Plata del almagre. In the long silence, Kenly heard a mutter of talk between Pablo and Don Rodrigo. The Almagres Mines were so called by reason of the red-ochre earth thereabouts, which likened that country to the Almagres district of Old Mexico. The red earth. The words took a sinister turn in Kenly's brain. He found Devore sidling up to his side, insistent.

"Heard that, cap'n? Ain't too late yet. We could treat with them Injuns. That gal ain't unwilling; look at her! Not by a damn sight she ain't—"

"Go to hell," snapped Kenly in an undertone, and followed it with hot words that rivermen could pour forth. Devore grinned viciously.

"If you won't foller your knife, you can foller your nose. You got something there you don't get rid of so easy; marked, that's what you are! All right. But you'll talk turkey 'fore you're done."

Devore rejoined his fellows. Red Wolf had turned and was striding back to his warriors, who were mounting. The crone was hastening up the hill. She came grinning, cackling, giving the bracelet to the girl, who examined it and then slipped it upon her arm. The heavy metal gleamed like dull fire in the sunlight.

"Almagre silver!" she said to Don Rodrigo. "You heard? Now am I foolish, eh?"

"To horse!" said Don Rodrigo. The Comanches were riding away. "Get the beasts, Pablo. Forward to Bejar!"

Kenly went with Pablo to lend a hand saddling and bringing up the animals.

"How far now?" he asked, as they worked. Pablo snarled a little, baring his teeth.

"One camp more, *señor. Caramba!* Matters have been like horns in a bag; but that knife made one good stroke for us. You may yet wish the lady had gone with the Indio, rather than the knife. Women, like men, are as God made them—and sometimes worse. Believe nothing of what you may see in that direction. She may appear to hold her finger ready, but she takes the ring to the jeweler first."

Later, when he brought up her horse and handed her to the saddle, she laughed gaily at him, brightly, intimately.

"What a dark look, my Hugo! You are sorry to have lost your knife?"

"Perhaps. You're sorry not to have followed it?"

"Oh, la, la!" She laughed heartily. "One must see what one has. I am not for common men, me—"

Then they were off, striking on after a couple of hours into a traveled road. And Kenly kept to himself that day.

He bedded that night with a pistol borrowed from Don Rodrigo, but nothing happened. And, in the fading twilight of the next day, they came into the city of the many names, past the missions of Capistrano and Conception, past the ditches and fields and the brown monks, and the half-breeds and the descendants of the Canary Islanders who had colonized this place.

Not much of a city, in many ways. Twenty years ago it had been desolate and abandoned, the victim of Mexican massacre and fury, and it had scarce recovered now. Yet, for Texas, it was a great place. Shabby scattered huts gave place to poplars and thicker growths, then grew a low jumble of flat-roofed buildings sentineled by the noble tower of a great church showing on before. Bugles sounded on the right, and Don Rodrigo waved his hand gaily, with eager word for Kenly, beside him.

"The old Alamo mission, now a strong fortress, *señor*. The guard is being changed. *Viva Mexico!* We have arrived. General Cos is on the alert. All is well. The tower yonder is the great church of San Fernando de Bejar."

"Which may expect those two candles which I vowed," muttered old Matilde. "But having come this far, I'll wait to buy them with silver from San Saba."

They crossed the bend of the river, curving and curving sharply, and Don Rodrigo touched spurs to his horse.

"I must find a surgeon. Pablo, take charge of the three Americans and Don Hugo, until I see you again."

Then he was gone, veering quickly away, with the two women riding after him. And if Kenly sought a look, a wave of farewell, from the girl, it was in vain. He heard Pablo coming up beside him, speaking in confidence.

"I know not what will come of all this; the dog wags his tail for what you'll give him. But I am Pablo Saccaplata, and my sister is honest as I am; she's no Conchita, any more than the latter is the *capitan's* cousin. I shall say nothing about the knife, my *señor*. Don Santiago Bowie was well liked here in San Antonio."

Kenly's eyes warmed. There was something in that earnest pocked countenance which was comforting as a coin in the pocket.

So they rode into San Antonio de Bejar, for well or ill.

CHAPTER VI

DOÑA MARIA

A N OLDER, wiser Kenly paced the streets of Bejar, a man desperate, hemmed in on all sides by fate, tricked and betrayed and schooling himself to patience, to waiting. Gone was Hugh Kenly, riverman. The old life lay dead behind him, dead as Jim Bowie.

A visored cap whose leather was flimsy as pasteboard, cotton jacket, ill-cut cotton trousers, coarse and clumsy brogans—his own stout foot gear promptly stolen—orders and drill which he knew already but must learn over in Mexican style. He was close to the bottom now. Officer's rank? It was to laugh. A private, and lucky to be that. He took satisfaction from the burning curses of Devore, whom he met at times.

"A dollar and a quarter a day, is it? Yes, and keep yourself in food and liquor, with every stitch you wear sold ag'in your pay so you never have a copper coming. And for this I gave up eleven dollars a month, United States, and keep! To hell with it. But I'm keeping an eye on you, all the same. We're due to make a bust, you and me."

To which Kenly said nothing. He was beyond curses, even. He had seen not a soul he knew, save Pablo occasionally.

The street called Acequia, fronted on one side by the solid façades of the tenements called Zambrano Row, on the other by the walled premises of two handsome gardened residences, lay sombre and silent this night. Kenly, assigned to service, was pacing out his period of sentry go, guarding the dark street.

The moon, now at the half, should be shining; but dank mist so dampened it that light and shadow was all one silver gray. The street itself never had a glim. The deep windows of Zambrano Row were shuttered closely. The embrasured doors were closed to eye and ear. What passed within those walls, Kenly knew not; the privacy of rank was to be upheld by a soldier walking guard.

Kenly strode forth and back on blistered feet, galled by the clumsy brogans. Ahead of him, a door of the Row suddenly opened; a black-shawled figure issued from the entrance. Its scuttling step rang familiar to his brain. With quick impulse he clumped in pursuit, overtook it, spoke swiftly.

"*Señora!*"

"Out with you, rascal!" came the indignant squeak. "The old cat prefers young mice, it is true, but I am a bit toothless to make good play." She demonstrated with a grin from the gathered canopy of her shawl; a grin that changed into a gape of astonishment and recognition. "Oh, it's you, is it! Shameless, to accost an old woman in the very street."

Matilde it was, and to Kenly at this moment she was beautiful enough.

"You mistake, *señora*. I confess that—"

"God save you from disappointment!" she gabbled on. "I know nothing for you. I care nothing for you. Confession is for the priest."

"I want to ask about Doña Maria. She is well?"

"But you have seen her, of course?

"No," snapped Kenly, with anger rising at her tone of mockery.

"What a strange thing!" and she cackled as she surveyed him. "I thought you were dining with her at this moment. You are, of course, a general at the very least?"

"Answer my question. Where is she? Where's Don Rodrigo? Where can I find them?"

"You have something to say to them, perhaps?" Her hag's laugh rang out again. "No doubt you'll find Don Rodrigo where he is, when he sends for you. And she likewise. To be sure, the *capitan's* whereabouts is none of my affair. As for her—well, watch the second door from here, and you'll learn more than I can tell you. *Adios.*"

She went shuffling away. Kenly, on his reluctant beat, kept eye and ear for the door. Perhaps twenty minutes later, it opened abruptly. Two figures came out; military cloak, woman's cloak. Kenly recognized her figure at once. He halted, turned.

"*Señorita!* Doña Maria!"

"Out of the way, you dog," exclaimed the officer angrily.

"Wait, Leon, wait!" broke out the voice of Doña Maria. "He means no harm; he is one of our recruits from Louisiana. Walk on; leave me a moment with him, Leon. I will follow." She turned to Kenly. "Well, *señor?* What is it you wish?"

"Merely to remind you that I am here, and to ask after Don Rodrigo."

Her foot tapped impatience on the stones.

"I know very well that you are here. Don Rodrigo? I have forgotten him; ah, yes, the brave *capitan*, of course!" She laughed a little, then softened. "Wait, *señor*; I cannot talk with you in the street. You see, I have not yet spoken with General Cos. I am going now to the Veramendi house; he is there. Maybe tonight, *Hugo mio*; who knows? You are not an officer; I understand. Well, I'll take care of that, never fear. *Adios!*"

And with a twinkle of white ankles she hastened on across the street to the corner where her officer escort was posted.

Kenly looked after her, then with an irritated oath shouldered his musket anew and kept to his beat. He had just reached the other end when he himself was accosted by a figure emerging from a shadowed nook. It was Matt Devore.

"What are you doing here?" Kenly demanded. The other spat, and laughed.

"I've broken bounds, if you want to know. Me and this *hombre*," and Devore jerked thumb at a companion in the shadows. "I seen you talking with cloak and hood; the same doxie, eh? She had the ankles anyhow; had a deal more for you, mebbe, or will have. I wish they'd put me on this beat—I'm ripe for anything! What'd she tell you?"

"Nothing for you," rasped Kenly. "Get to hell out of here."

"Come, you wouldn't report a pardner," and Devore stepped in close. "Listen, Jim Bowie used to hang out here in the Ve-ramendi house—married into it. His friends'd like to know what I know, see? And they ain't Mexicans neither." Suddenly his tone changed. "Hey, d'you know them Texans are a-raising hell? Cos is going to fort the place ag'in 'em; he's doing it now, if you've seen the work. We're like to be ketched on the wrong side of the fence. Then what?"

"Clear out, you drunken roustabout. Your talk doesn't scare me—"

"You're scared plenty or you wouldn't be here," gibed the other. "There's been fighting, I tell you, and the damned country is up. They'll be coming. Let's clear out, Kenly; we can sneak guns and powder, and slide for the San Saba country. By cripes, if I could lay hands on that gal once, I bet she'd talk! She knows where that map is—I know good and well you ain't got it. All right, surly shanks. I'm having a fling tonight if I hang for it. This *amigo* knows a place or two. See you later."

DEVORE, OBVIOUSLY, had been imbibing freely. With his companion, he went lurching on down the street and both of them were swallowed up by the treacherous gloom. Kenly resumed his beat, scowling. He had another hour of it to serve out. From the Veramendi mansion came the drifting sound of music, a chorus of singing. Those damned officers were having a good time, eh?

Mischief was abroad this night, and every night, for discipline was a ghastly joke in these barracks. But things had tightened up in the past day or so, for some reason hard to say. Rumors were abroad on all sides—wild rumors of fight and flight, of Texans who slew and slew, of armies moving north from Mexico, of strange sights and sounds. One man swore he had seen the face of the President and Dictator, Santa Anna, at the window of a rolling carriage. But Santa Anna was far south—

Abruptly, the false peace of the street was broken by a woman's high and frightened voice. Kenly swung around. He saw her figure break forth from the shadows into which Doña Maria had vanished. With a glimpse of white ankles, a flutter of draperies, she ran desperately across the street, ran on with intent aim. Kenly followed. She was Doña Maria, of course; he had no other thought. He broke into a run, to intercept the pursuit that bayed up after her.

She darted for a street, a side street that was no street after all. It was only a short blind lane, ending at a wall set with a door. She flung herself at it; a hard-latched or locked door, for she beat at the planks vainly, then turned at the sound of Kenly's steps.

"No, no, for the love of God!" Then she fell to her knees, suppliant and exhausted. Kenly had one glimpse of her white face, then swung around.

The passage echoed to exultant oaths and the hot breath of oncoming beasts, the scuffling tread of their running feet. Anything might be expected in a frontier town garrisoned by famished men. In the murk of the lane, a glint from the moon gave just a ray of light. Figures like slinking wolves slipping forward. A heavy fragment of stone fanned Kenly's cheek and crashed resoundingly against the door.

The tall hammer of his musket had already clicked a warning. His voice was drowned in a torrent of oaths. Another stone splintered at his shoulder. The air was filled with them, men were howling at him—he threw his musket to his cheek and pulled trigger.

With the roar, came the concussion of a terrific blow as though between the eyes. It toppled him upon his knees, blinded him with blood and sickening pain. For a little he was aware of things. Shouts and oaths growing fainter, murmurings and quick soft words above him.

Then he went floating, floating, conscious only of his bursting head, of agony under the exploration of distant fingers. Then darkness.

Darkness, for a long while, and dull, merciful numbness. Time interminable; full years, it seemed. Soup and water introduced between his lips now and again, dressings and bandages changed, low murmurs and cool soft fingers. But always darkness, until the day that the bandages were lessened and his eyes freed.

The daylight blinded him for a while, so that he kept his eyes closed until he could bear it. Then he looked up at her, at the girl watching him. A pallet in a small, whitewashed room where other pallets lay crowded. No, it was not Doña Maria.

"Be quiet, *señor*, if you please. You're getting well."

Kenly stared at her. He spoke thickly, for his throat was dry.

"And you? Who are you?"

YOUNG DARK eyes, soft with tenderness, bent above him; cool fingers touched his forehead, the rough stubble of beard on his chin. The smiling glory of her face was a lovely thing to see. Then she straightened up, leaned back on her stool, and laughed aloud.

"I am the *señorita* Andrea Josefa de Candelaria, *señor*. It is Pablo Saccaplata who is my half-brother. You know, the soldier Pablo—"

"Josefa! You are the Josefa he mentioned—yes, yes. Where am I?"

"In my room and my mother's, *señor*. There is no hospital in San Antonio. We owe you so much—I owe you so much! Do you remember the other night? Ah, those white Apaches!" Her dark eyes blazed in a face that was suddenly white. "The door was locked; I had nowhere to run. And they would have killed you had you not fired."

"What did this?" Kenly lifted his hand, touched the bandages, winced. "A stone?"

"No; the gun burst, *señor*. It shot, but it burst, also. And you did not hold it tightly to the shoulder. The bullet went, it is true, but the stock was dashed into your face."

"My nose is broken?"

"So the surgeon said, *señor*; much broken. He came and looked at you, and did what he could; it was not much. Then he tied you up and left you to my care, which is as should be. At least, God guided your bullet; you can rest easy with that! Ah, if it had been a cannon loaded with grape!" And she flared suddenly with anger. "If I also had but had a musket!"

"You mean I shot one of those rascals?"

"Yes, you did. *Viva!* Only you did not kill him; you shot him through the leg. A soldier named Mateo. An Americano."

"Mateo? Oh, Matthew! Matt Devore, was it?"

"Something like that. He won't chase another girl in a hurry. He made a bad error; I'm not the kind for him and his friends. But on these streets at night a girl should carry a knife as big and long as the knife of Don Santiago Bowie."

The name jerked at Kenly. So Devore had dropped to that bullet! He had stood between Devore and his spoil of lust; another score chalked up for settlement with an animal already vindictive. Now another score was brought to his mind; that chalked up in red to spell Jim Bowie, dead in New Orleans.

"You know—you knew Santiago Bowie?"

"Of course, *señor*. He lived here in the Veramendi house. *Que lastima!* What a sorrow was his! Wife and two children, all carried away by the pestilence. I remember him in my prayers as I shall always remember you. He is a good man, too—"

"You spoke of a knife."

"Of course; his own, *señor*, and what a knife! Handle set with silver from the mines he found and lost again, and a blade that would stick an ox. A knife well used, too. With it he once saved me as you did with your gun and body. A true *caballero* and my friend—for my blood is as good as those of the Veramendis."

As she spoke of Bowie, her lovely features glowed with animation. Then she caught up basin and cloth from the floor.

"I must bathe your poor face again, my brave one, and wet the bandages."

"My brave one!" Tartly, shrewdly, were the words echoed. "And in her very bed!"

The girl turned in surprise. Someone had come into the room with a quick inrush like a burst of hot sunshine when a door is opened. And like sunshine she was; Doña Maria, no less, radiant and sparkling, with old Matilde peering in from the entrance. The visitor's voice rang out again, acidly.

"So here I find you, Don Hugo—a pretty scene, indeed a scene that goes to my heart. Well, you are of the ranks, not an officer. True and doubly true, so make the most of her bed and her pretty self, my American—"

Josefa straightened up, white where the other was flushed. She grated:

"You mistake, Doña Conchita," and the name held a biting scorn. "The bed is not mine, but his; I share my mother's bed. There is other report of you, I believe."

"He, he!" The cackle of old Matilde rose quick and sharp in glee. "One who goes fishing must not mind a wetting. He, he! That was a good one, that was."

"Silence, gutter girl!" Doña Maria remembered, no doubt, that she was a lady; the hand thrust into her bosom came out empty. Her brows lifted. "What can such as you know of me? You are ignorant. Because Santiago Bowie once was kind to you, your head was turned." She swung around to Kenly. "You know who she is? A servant, a camp woman, a girl who follows the soldiers and washes their dirty shirts and hopes that some day an officer will notice her—"

"You seem to know the way of it," said Josefa. Doña Maria ignored her.

"And for such as this you left your post and got injured, squabbling over a girl of the streets!" She brushed forward and bent over him, her hand touching his brow, her face suddenly alluring, radiant. "Or did you mistake her for me, my Hugo?"

"NATURALLY. AT first—"

"So I told General Cos," she broke in, laughing. "You'll not be punished; not when you've suffered for me, *amigo!* The man you shot is a liar. Everything is understood. My poor Hugo!" Her hand brushed his forehead lightly. "I came to you when I heard of it. You must stay here until healed, yes. Then I'll send for you." She straightened up and turned. "See that this *caballero* is well taken care of, my girl. He is not what you think; he is not for you, but for your betters. *Adios*, my Hugo!"

And she was gone, like a ray of hot blistering sunlight out of a cool room, leaving Kenly flushed and uneasy, the dark, slim, lovely girl flushed and angry. She looked down at Kenly now, with a stormy pride and disdain and questioning in her dark eyes.

"She is a friend of your, *señor?*"

"Ask Pablo." Kenly smiled thinly. "She came from New Orleans with Don Rodrigo. Have you not heard?"

"Pablo talks less than he might, at times. So you took me for her? Why, I would not let her touch the edge of my skirt! And you took me for her!"

"Yes, I did," Kenly said bluntly. "Why not? It was dark. Any girl deviled by those beasts would have drawn the same help. Say no more of it."

She regarded him for a moment, her head on one side. Suddenly she smiled.

"Ah, your words are like bullets; they are well aimed, they fly true. Now let me bathe your face. Both Pablo and I are at your service forever."

Kenly saw her with new eyes, after the departure of the other; saw her with new and clearer vision. Vividly white and black she was, the loveliness of her face changeful as a mirroring pool that reflects the clouds and records every tender passage of the airs. After the hot sun of the other woman, her cooling touch was a very wisp of twilight, and grateful to the senses.

Kenly smiled and fell asleep, contentedly.

Later, toward evening, the mother came, and he looked up at her amazedly. She was a grenadier of a woman, with mustache dark upon her lip, a hoarse voice like that of a crow. A hard, alert, practical woman, yet gentle enough and very tender in the eyes.

Pablo came and sat down beside the pallet, with his homely grin.

"Ah, I have been busy!" he sighed. "Working. Wait till you see the Alamo, where the good priests once walked.

"We're tearing down half of it and building a ramp for heavy artillery to go on the roof. And the worthy *capitan* is gone, too."

"Eh?" said Kenly. "You mean our Don Rodrigo?"

"He, assuredly." Pablo glanced over his shoulder, found the others out of the room, and winked. "What did I tell you? Ordered away to Monclova in Mexico, where he'll get better treatment for his festered wound. So they say, anyhow. But he went alone, you comprehend? And you, *señor*, are to be brought to General Cos as soon as you're well. Those are the orders now." Pablo scratched his head. "It must be the San Saba affair. *Caramba!* The devil certainly hides behind the cross."

"And what do you mean by that, *amigo?*"

Pablo shrugged. "That Doña Maria. The business is changed now; it has too little of the *capitan* in it and too much of the *doña.* He is a man of his word, but she's a woman of many words. She's well received by the general—you understand? Trust her. She doesn't fling water from a window without looking first. And that cursed Indian!"

Kenly frowned at all this. "The young chief, you mean? He's not here?"

"Coming; they've given him safe conduct and an escort. Pray to the saints that the *capitan* returns ere long. He's a man of influence and family. Even the general would not trifle with him. Ah, well!" Pablo sighed. "I don't know what to make of it all. The world must be coming to an end. Some say that Santa Anna has come secretly. All say there is fighting everywhere outside this town alone. These accursed Tejanos! I'm glad you're an American, *señor*. These people of Texas—well, they are hard to keep down, whether they're of your blood or mine."

Kenly laughed a little, and Pablo said no more.

CHAPTER VII

KENLY'S CHOICE

PABLO STAMPED into the room where Kenly was resting.

"General Cos will see you at once, *señor*," he said.

The bandages were but now removed. Kenly, gingerly fingering his hurts, found them fairly well healed, but the surface that remained was odd and strange to his touch. Josefa surveyed him anxiously.

"You must not handle your face, do you understand?" she cautioned him. "The bone is still soft. The hurt was deep."

"I must look at myself, Josefa. Have you a glass?"

"A mirror, *señor?* What would we do with a mirror? A girl like me, who washes the shirts of soldiers, does not use one." She vented a hard little laugh. "Well, I've washed your shirt, at least."

"Bah! Is my nose crooked?"

"How do I know, since I didn't see it before the damage was done?" she parried. "At least, it's nothing to be ashamed of. Eh, Pablo?"

Pablo looked a trifle startled. "*Caramba!* If we were all as handsome as Don Rodrigo, what were the use of good looks? Handsome is as handsome does," he added, then gave Kenly a scrutiny. "*Bravo, señor;* a lucky stroke was that! If ever you stole a horse, you can talk with the owner now. There are men who would prize that stroke, *caballero;* it is as good as a pardon."

Then sudden anxiety came into his face.

"They said you were to come to the general at once, *señor*. And Josefa too. I do not like this, not by half."

A cry broke from the girl. "To the general? I am to go?"

"Yes. To the Veramendi house; that's headquarters, until the work is finished at the Alamo. And what the devil does he want with her?" grumbled Pablo, with a glance after the flustered, scurrying girl. "He may give her a peso, but there are too many eyes in such a place, for a girl like her. Nothing more than a peso, I hope!"

They set forth with scant delay. And all the way to the Veramendi house was hedged with eyes; but for Kenly, rather than for the girl, as he became conscious. It must be his face; the eyes were sometimes astonished and sometimes mirthful, and he knew the story of his hurt must have traveled far.

They came to the great house at last, and the premises inside the sentry-guarded gate were aglitter with uniforms—queerly aglitter, with officers looking important and aides dashing about for no obvious reason. Here was all the air of something deep and mysterious.

Pablo was quickly dropped. Ushered on through an anteroom where the eyes of officers were not for him alone, Kenly found himself, with the girl, thrust across a threshold and posted with the words:

"The two for whom you asked, general. General Don Martin Perfecto de Cos."

The aide saluted again, wheeled about and in exit closed the door behind him. Kenly looked, not at one person, but at three seated here.

Doña Maria, sitting very much at ease, and two men behind the heavy mahogany table. They, also, were at ease so far as dazzling regalia would permit, with glory of gold and scarlet. And a fourth person—a private soldier standing with a countenance like a grotesque monkey-mask, featured as it was by a whitish paint band and a nose flattened askew, Kenly stared and then, in compassion, he shifted his gaze. The figure imitated, glanced back at him. He was looking at himself in a pier glass. The whitish band was the skin bleached by bandages; the nose was his nose. His fingers had truly reported, but the mirror was brutally honest.

"Come! What is your name?"

Kenly wakened from his stupefaction. He had been sharply addressed by General Cos, the heavier of the two officers. A man of abundant coarse, obstinate black hair, thick arched brows, oval face with straight nose and pointed chin. Not an unpleasant, although portly man; the face was intelligent; of a shrewdness that might mean anything or nothing.

"Hugo Kenly."

"*Dios!* It is he after all!" Doña Maria laughed in amusement that bit deep. "Why, his own mother would not know him, assuredly!"

The general smiled, leaned over to her, and spoke rapidly under his breath. The other officer, who had been gazing fixedly at Josefa, addressed her.

"Come, little one, and what is your name?"

H E S A T higher than General Cos. He was of longer body, his smooth-shaven face of high forehead and fine hair brushed back. The large, full eyes and firm lips marked a face graven by passions; intolerance, craft, bold self-indulgence. He, too, wore the epaulets of a general.

"Andrea Josefa de Candelaria, *señor*," replied the girl simply. Doña Maria turned.

"She is impudent! Girl, say Your Excellency. Ah, what ignorance!"

General Cos smiled indulgently. "His Excellency will pardon you, girl. Do you know who condescends to question you? His Excellency himself, El Presidente, General Don Antonio Lopez de Santa Anna."

Santa Anna! Kenly felt the name chill him with surprise and foreboding. The dictator of Mexico, the man who had swept

Red Wolf swerved and snatched up Josefa.

aside all state rights and made himself supreme—and he, Hugh
Kenly, summoned as if for conference, to a tribunal of Santa
Anna, General Cos, and the fiercely radiant Doña Maria! This
last sat there like a glowing fury, her blue eyes darting venom
at Josefa.

"A condescension, upon my word!" she spat. "And all wasted,
Your Excellency."

"Better bestowed on yourself, eh?" thought Kenly, as he eyed
the beauty. Something in her manner, in her glowing regard,
brought a shiver to him. But Santa Anna smiled at Josefa with
an indulgence neither fatherly nor fraternal.

"But you are lovely, my little one," he said musingly. His eyes
traversed her; they were oblivious of all the others. Kenly sensed
that Josefa flinched under this regard. "I perceive, my general,
that I shall have to change my headquarters to Bejar at an early
date. If this little one is of the camp, as you say—then it's time
I took to the field myself. She lives here?"

"Yes, Your Excellency," said Cos. "With her stepmother. Her
half-brother is a private in the garrison; one Saccaplata."

"So. You have a lover, little one? Perhaps the man beside you?"

"No!" cried Josefa hotly. "No, Your Excellency."

"Be careful!" Santa Anna laughed at her flare. "*Caspita!* His nose is out of joint already. We'll find a better man for you some day. Well, well, there is business, my general; let us settle it first of all."

Cos nodded and bent his regard on the American.

"Your name is Kenly. Yes, Don Rodrigo Estramadura has spoken of you. You came here with more in view than simple service in the ranks; but this was necessary for a time. Well, that is all ended now—"

A knock interrupted. The door opened, and from the threshold an aide saluted.

"My general, the Indian is here."

General Cos, toying with papers before him, nodded. "Send him in. Wait; take this girl and see that she's conducted safely outside." Cos turned to Josefa. "His Excellency was pleased to be interested, upon learning how you nursed this man of the broken nose. You will be rewarded later. You may go."

The way was momentarily blocked. Red Wolf, the Comanche, was already in the room, wearing leggings but no paint, unarmed, his black eyes sweeping the room, flitting from person to person, pausing at last upon Josefa. She brushed past him for the doorway, and his eyes followed her until the door closed; so did the eyes of Santa Anna. Doña Maria glanced from one to the other, and laughed harshly.

"Reward?" she echoed. "I think, my general, she has already had reward enough—but she did not even thank you. She is a child without manners. Well, here is the *capitan grande* of the Comanche nation, Red Wolf, the war chief."

"Welcome," said General Cos, then looked at Kenly. "As you know, *señor*, we deal with the matter of the San Saba mines. Here is the map, of which you know also. Mexico desires to re-locate and re-open those mines of hers."

"Doubtless," commented Kenly.

"It is of importance to bring His Excellency here on a flying visit. But there is a more serious matter; that of the man you are said to have killed in New Orleans."

Kenly started. Again? Bowie still pursuing him?

"That was a mistake, sir. The killing was accidental. It took place far from Mexican soil, in any case—"

"No matter. Apologies following a blow do not mend it," Cos said drily. He drummed upon the table, then spoke abruptly. "We are accused of harboring a murderer."

"I don't understand this—"

"I'll be plain. The man you struck down was married into the Veramendi family. You are now a soldier in the service of Mexico. The Veramendi family see no reason why you should not be taken to Mexico City and tried for murder—perhaps shot out of hand."

THE ATMOSPHERE of the room had tensed. Kenly felt the eyes upon him, surveying him curiously; those of Doña Maria, of the two generals, of the impassive Indian. He himself was the center of everything. He felt as though some net were closing about him. It came to him from those other watching brains, so intent upon him. He sensed falsehood, treachery, some monstrous lie gathering imponderable forces around him.

"Why go into this matter?" he asked, a little scornfully.

"Because it is serious. There is a way out. The man Bowie was a Mexican citizen, although rebellious. You may have served Mexico in killing him, but the Veramendi family insist that Mexico punish you. He was deeply loved by them, and Mexico cannot disregard their influence. Is it not so, Your Excellency?"

"You speak well," and Santa Anna nodded. "Too many traitors are supporting these rebels already; we do not desire to alienate more of the old families here."

"But there is a way out," insisted General Cos smoothly. "This way carries to the New Almagres mines of the San Saba. Now,

I should think, you need have no fear of being recognized by anyone on the outside, eh?"

"It would be unlikely," said Kenly.

"Good; the very point," and Cos smiled. "You shot a man of your own race who loves you not. He might send out word about you. We cannot have you depart alone on the mission we have in mind."

"You're talking in circles," Kenly broke out curtly. "Come to the point. What do you want of me?"

"A decision. Will you go as prisoner to Mexico City, or will you establish your worth by taking an expedition to the San Saba? You'll return with a few pack loads of silver. Thanks to Doña Maria, we have arranged with Red Wolf that the Indian country will be open to you."

Cos paused, glancing at the papers before him as though to refresh his mind, We have arranged! The words struck into Kenly with sinister meaning; later he remembered them more acutely. Then Cos pursued.

"His people control the mines. As a Comanche, he cares nothing about the silver. His mother was an Apache. For yourself, I guarantee that your case will be settled with the Vera-mendi family by His Excellency. I'll appoint you a lieutenant on the spot, and upon your return you shall become a captain. Doña Maria has asked this favor. I grant it."

"Oh, la!" and Doña Maria laughed. "A captain, eh? Come, that will be interesting, very! Will it not, my Hugo?"

Kenly did not look at her. He ignored her words, her eyes.

"But these Texans?" he demanded. "If there is war—"

General Cos broke into a laugh, and looked at his brother-in-law, the thin and sardonic Santa Anna.

"Oh, the Texans!" he repeated, using the American word instead of the Spanish *Tejanos*. "They are to laugh! They fear to come near Bejar, and when the time is ripe I'll crush them with one regiment of dragoons and a couple of cannon. Wait until they have gathered all together; then they'll die all at once.

Meantime, I keep idle men at work fortifying the city. However, if you're taken by the Texans you'll be shot; they'll not forgive you for killing Bowie."

Santa Anna intervened brusquely.

"I have no more time to waste here. *Señor*, do you go south with me or north with others? I hear you are a brave man. As president and general, I can be severe or generous. The answer is for you to make, at once."

Kenly shrugged. The net had been deftly drawn about him. The Veramendi family? He doubted this. He doubted everything. But he had no choice.

He hated every person in this room. The tense atmosphere reeked with falsity. Something here of Doña Maria's conniving; and the impassive, silent Indian was of it also. A cruel amusement in the blue eyes of the girl. In those of Santa Anna, the interested, slyly attentive look of a cat watching a mouse. The whole room was like a bomb set with slow but certain fuse.

General Cos spoke again. "Unfortunately, Don Rodrigo Estramadura, by reason of his wound, is deprived of the honor of this first expedition to the San Saba. That honor is your due, and so is offered you. Only you and he, outside these quarters, have seen this map. A matter of this kind is best handled with gloves. Which way, *señor?*"

"To the San Saba, certainly," said Kenly. And knew what he was going to do, as he spoke.

"Good. You will report to the Alamo at once for lieutenant's uniform and remain there. At eight tomorrow morning you will depart in charge of the expedition. You will find everything arranged. Here; take this copy of the map, and guard it well." He extended a folded paper to Kenly, who took it. Then he turned to the Comanche. "Here is the lieutenant who leads. Report to him at the Alamo, at eight in the morning."

The Indian's fathomless black eyes shot with mysterious glints. They focused upon Kenly with a contact, a tensity, that was almost physical. The steady gaze made naught of space, of flesh or bone. Then the Comanche uttered his only words: "Captain Flatnose."

Doña Maria tittered. A smile flickered upon the long countenance of Santa Anna, and twitched at the mustache of General Cos, who nodded and gave quittance.

"*Vaya con Dios!* Go with God, lieutenant."

Kenly saluted and turned to the door. He left the room. He was just closing the door behind him when he heard Doña Maria's voice, carried on a burst of laughter:

"Captain Flatnose! Oh, *Santo Dios*, what a face!"

CHAPTER VIII

EXPEDITION

CAPTAIN FLATNOSE. Well, why not? It was a good enough name for a man damned. A harsh laugh broke from Kenly, as he headed through town for the Alamo.

He noted that the leading streets were being barricaded, the walls rimming the flat house-roofs being loop-holed. These measures, portending of siege and active war, concerned him little; he was going on the morrow—and not returning.

His brain was active, bursting with suggestions and retrospect; he was proof against glances and remarks, compassion and ridicule, as he strode along. Apparently the prospective outcome of his mission was very simple, so simple as to have escaped the urbane General Cos, even the merry Doña Maria. She had cozened him cleverly.

Thank heaven that, at the last, he had given a good nose in behalf of a mere wanton! He was spared this trick of fate, else the disfigurement would have been galling. That Josefa and not the jade Conchita might justly claim the sacrifice, was some satisfaction. And once out of this place, he was gone for good. To the devil with all of them!

He came to the outskirts of town. Beyond lay the outskirts of Bejar, and just across the river, the Alamo walls uplifted, just now a hive of activity, for certain of the outer walls and buildings were being torn down and piled in a ramp by which artillery might be lifted to the roof of the stone chapel.

The Alamo—strange name! Once garrisoned by a troop of

Indian fighters, the Flying Company of Alamo de Parras down in Mexico, it had retained the name, and was now simply the Alamo. For a long time it had been devoted to military purposes. Outlying to the left of the high stone chapel was the present barracks. The wide walled area was two acres in extent, premises one time dedicated by labor of priest, Indian, soldier and settler, enclosed stables, courtyards, ruins. Kenly eyed them all moodily. These precincts of venerable disarray, livened by the garrison, interested him now only as a point of departure. He was heartily sick of the whole place.

He obtained his uniform. The other officers took charge of him, celebrating his appointment. Two of them were Americans, sons of settlers below the line. Kenly found himself lifted to sudden gaiety, joviality. Not until dinner came, and darkness, was he free to cross town again and search out Josefa.

She was not there, nor the grenadier, nor Pablo; all gone, and the massive door locked. He turned away, uneasy, disturbed, and went back again to the Alamo and at length to sleep. His face hurt a little, burned by the sun.

Morning came, and Pablo shaking him awake, wearing corporal's insignia, but the pock-marked visage was glum none the less.

"Just time for breakfast, my lieutenant," said Pablo. Kenly came to one elbow.

"Josefa? I must find her, say farewell."

"No need," said Pablo, and made a gesture of caution toward the others around. "Now the arrow flies," he added cryptically, and departed.

Kenly breakfasted, shaved, donned his lieutenant's uniform. A dragoon summoned him. Once again, as he came to the outer court beyond the chapel, where cannon were being mounted, the stifling sense of futility crowded upon him, the feel of having been wound in a net. "We have arranged—"

For here his expedition was assembled and mounting, and Josefa was here, with her mother and half a dozen other women. Fifteen pack mules, with complement of muleteers, a horse for himself, the road for the women, boots for the men; ten of them under Pablo. Devore and his two companions were of the ten, Devore limping and gaunt, venomous of eye, thinned by his hurt, yet bearing himself with an alacrity which was almost exultation. Why? Again Kenly found himself confused, groping for the force at work here which he could not discover. He went to Josefa and her mother with questions.

"Why? It was ordered. All women must accompany their men," said Josefa, and laughed. "Pablo is a corporal; well, why not? I long to see the prairies!"

No time for more. Orders? Whose orders? Kenly thought of the curling lips of Doña Maria, who had stamped this slender lovely thing with the name of camp woman. Anger rose in him anew. He curtly returned the salute of Pablo, announcing all ready.

"Then march. My horse? Good."

As by magic, the figure of Red Wolf appeared, on an Indian pony; armed now with lance and bow, the knife hung to the belt of his leggings. The silvered haft had been wrapped with a buckskin thong.

The Comanche led, unasked, unasking, taking his place in the van as by right. A clump of officers, with two aides of the general, looked on and laughed as they talked together. Kenly saluted and followed the Indian, the motley procession trailing along behind him.

They headed up the road to the mill, and on out through the fields to the northwest. The soldiers afoot, with muskets and cartridge boxes, jested and broke into song. The women trudged valiantly; now and again changing, as the humor moved them, to muleback. A brown lot, these women, brown and thin and savage. Kenly knew not half the words that flew about nor the jests.

Out toward the horizon they swung, and Bejar fell behind into a mask of green trees, and the scattered farms were gone with the river. Noon approached, and Kenly ordered halt at a stream. Fresh food enough just now, but later it would be sun-dried beef chips and what might be sent by God. Kenly sought out the Comanche.

"You know of the place whither we go, *amigo?*"

"Yes. Where the bracelet came from," calmly said the chief.

"And how far?"

RED WOLF signed with sweep of arm, counted by erected thumb and fingers; with an air of disdain, since Kenly knew not the sign language, he vouchsafed to speak.

"Six day marches."

Forthwith he drew apart, to sit upon his haunches, aloof and lordly. His gaze wavered not. The black eyes fastened upon the group of women, the group dominated by the raucous voice and grenadier figure of the *señora*, Pablo's mother. Not upon her did the unwinking eyes settle, but upon the figure of Josefa in her plain yellow dress, her black mantilla.

Pablo came to Kenly, with pannikin and wooden spoon.

"A few beans for the lieutenant, from my mother," he said. "We have no fire, so if the lieutenant will not mind them cold—"

He squatted down. His voice came softly while Kenly ate, very softly.

"We're for the accursed silver, I know; we'll never get there. You'll never get there, or back either. Strangle the cock that crows!"

"Explain." Kenly darted a glance at him. "What mean you?"

"You know too much. I don't think Don Rodrigo has anything to do with this. You are not coming back, because you must run away; but do it in time! In a few days we'll be a long way from Bejar. But you must eat when the soup is hot, *señor*; the next day might be too late, Josefa wants to talk with you about it. Tonight, when we halt."

"You seem cursed gloomy," said Kenly.

"What else? We're all in the same boat. Those Americanos know about the map, so do I; the rest of those men are rascally fellows, poor soldiers, who could well be spared. It'll be either the Indians or the Tejanos."

Kenly caught his drift. "Nonsense; why, it'd be impossible! There are no Texans near here, are there?"

"God knows, not I," said Pablo. "There has been fighting. The dragoons have been whipped, and the general is preparing against an attack, so that he can kill all the Tejanos at once. You must run away quickly, and let us turn back for Bejar if that be possible. But come to our fire tonight; we cannot talk now.

"Josefa will have enough to say. Those three Americanos are dumb, stupid animals who suspect nothing. Why should I suspect anything?" He rose, took the pannikin again. "The vaquero can see the cows but he cannot see who drives them. May the devil requite that Doña Maria!"

Nooning was ended and march resumed. As Kenly rode, he thought upon Pablo's words. Yes; it was hard to see who drove the cows. Impossible to determine what lay behind all this. Had Santa Anna lied? Possibly. Not likely. It was all confusion.

All but his own part. He had planned to cut loose and strike for the Louisiana border, the settlements, anywhere. He could get back into Louisiana, with this new face of his, and shake off the dust of Texas forever. What of the others?

Kenly frowned. He could decide on nothing. Pablo's suspicions seemed absurd. General Cos was sending them after the silver, which he wanted—or was he? "We have arranged—" What was arranged with that dour, silent Comanche, whose black eyes glittered ever upon Josefa? What had passed between the Indian and Doña Maria? Kenly shivered a little at the thought, at the suggestion. Why was the Indian now intent upon Josefa, with passionate, unwinking gaze? It boded ill. The whole thing had a darkly sinister aspect as of cloaked deviltry in suspense.

"I'll clear out in good time," Kenly decided. "Pablo's advice scores dead center. The others can turn back safely. What's Devore doing here? Singular! Unless Pablo can be right about that as well. Can I leave them, if they're doomed? The affair's a cursed embroglio. Some deep rascality behind it."

He thrust everything away to await the evening, and information.

WITH SUNSET they came upon water, and struck camp. Little fires flickered up into the gathering dusk. For a space Kenly stood talking with the men. The Americans were a surly, brutal lot. Devore made no mention of the past, of his wound, of anything; he ignored Kenly and began to muzzle one of the women openly. At this moment Pablo came up, all deference.

"Shall I build the lieutenant a fire and send my mother to cook for him? Or will he share our fire and what we may offer? On the march it is all like one family."

"I'll go with you," said Kenly, and followed. When he came to where the two women were at work over a small blaze, the grenadier blared greeting at him.

"Welcome, *señor*, will you be pleased to sit down? Everything you see is yours. With a little patience, you'll be served. Ha! The soldiery is as much a part of the army as a general, and more. The general keeps his skin safe, but I can handle a musket as well as any man."

The four were somewhat apart from the rest, Kenly noted. Their simple meal was soon ready and set forth. Josefa sat beside Kenly; in the ruddy firelight the girl looked troubled and anxious. Presently Kenly addressed her.

"You have something to say, my dear?"

She nodded. "Once, before Señora Bui died," and the name of Bowie fell softly from her lips, "I was often a guest in the Veramendi house. The servants there know me. One of them talked with me last night, in warning. The general expects to see none of us back, nor any silver either. Or, if not the general, at least there was talk among the officers, and much laughter."

"But it can't be so!" Kenly exclaimed. "Why, it's impossible—"

"Bah! It's plain enough," spat out the grenadier mother. "You, *señor*, had best leave us at the first opportunity and ride for your life. We'll risk the Texans and turn back. I'll tell the general and *El Presidente* to go look for their own silver. Order me and mine off with the soldiers, eh? Like common women of the camp. Well, we can make the best of it, but anger grows in the heart. I'm not afraid of them."

"I'm afraid, though," said the girl simply. "And that Indian! He's looking at me now. I can feel his eyes all the time."

Kenly glanced around. He caught a reflection of the firelight; the Comanche was there, like a wolf indeed, watching, waiting his time to strike.

"That Indian won't trouble us, my pet. I'll twist his neck like a chicken's." With her two hands figuratively disposed of Red Wolf. Then she smoothed the edges from her rasping voice. "And *El Presidente* looked at you too, eh? Well, that would be a grand thing for us if he married you!"

"What?" The girl shrank a little. "No, no; he is already married."

"Well, the last wife need not worry about the others," said her mother with hard practical sense. "That is for his account. All can be arranged. Why is he president if not to take what he can get?"

"Bah! You talk of absurdities," struck in Pablo with disdain.

"Indeed not! She is poor, but he is rich; and she has the old blood of Spain, which is more than Antonio Lopez de Santa Anna can boast. Well, we shall see. Perhaps if we ever get back to Bejar we shall end by living in Mexico City."

Kenly looked at the woman with astonishment and lack of comprehension. Then the girl beside him spoke with dark passion.

"Ah! I hope Don Santiago Bowie will come with his Tejanos and capture Bejar! Then it will be like the old days again. With Santa Anna there—"

"He's not there," said Pablo suddenly. "He left last night in a coach."

"No matter; others are as bad," said the girl. "When Texas is once more a state with its own laws, as it used to be, we'll breathe easier. That's what the Tejanos are going to fight for. God and Liberty!"

"God and Liberty!" cawed her mother in raucous mirth. "But think well of His Excellency just the same. An ass in golden trappings is better than a horse wearing a pack saddle."

In the morning, Kenly was roused from his blankets by a stir beside him. A fire began to crackle. He sat up to see Josefa there, and to meet her bright friendly smile, the touch of mockery in her words.

"You see, *señor*, I am only a girl of the camp! Well, I shall do my part, yes?"

She broke into a laugh, and Kenly with her. Then, as he passed to the water, Kenly saw that the Comanche was already up and watching. In their gaze his eyes were constant as the needle to the pole. But he remained silent as always. And today, Kenly noticed, the coppery features wore paint for the first time.

The march this day entered a rougher country, the onward vistas beckoning with mysteries, and Kenly looked to the out trail. Before another dawn he would be away. And Josefa? He frowned there. Well, she would understand. Pablo would understand. As for the Comanche, he might be disappointed, and might not. Whatever his thoughts were, or his instructions, they lay deep and voiceless like a stone at the bottom of a sunless pool.

But—Josefa? When Kenly's eyes fell upon her slender bounded beauty, upon the flash of the yellow dress under the mantilla, he frowned again. The simplicity of this girl was very lovely; it drew at him with invisible fingers. He had divined this fragile goodness in her from the first. No weakness in it; simplicity can be a very abrupt and terrible thing. And was he to leave her, then?

Perhaps this thought darkened everything. Yet, as the column advanced, the more Kenly felt that the trail sombered, even in the sunlight. Silence brooded vastly all around the horizon, silence broken only by the close sounds of hoof and sole, squeak of leather, piping voices and laughter; and this silence was like the brooding suspense of marshaled thunderheads. The air, to him, warned of quickening event.

NOON CAME, the nooning which was to be his last. Red Wolf led them to cunning water deep in a trickling wash below them, fringed thick with cottonwoods. They had barely unsaddled, when, without an instant's warning, the storm broke. Broke, with only one sharp yelp from the *señora*.

Amazingly sudden was the crackle of high fierce yells, the hiss and patter of arrows from the shrubbery. And in this instant of clamor and battle, as the musket of Pablo roared forth, the worst happened.

Red Wolf vaulted astride with one bound, brought down his hand, and his pony leaped. In full course he swerved, leaned far over, and snatched up Josefa where she stood. Past Kenly in a brush of air, a thrust of the lance that missed, and plunging headlong into the brush.

With that one picture in his eyes and the one thought in his brain, Kenly was in the saddle. His horse leaped after, with frantic spur, leaped and hurtled into the brush and down the sharp slope into the wash. A red face, painted, rose, and Kenly pistoled the leaping figure in midair. Thank heaven, Pablo had charged his pistols! He let the empty weapon fall—there was another in the other holster—and settled himself to the pursuit. Everything else fell behind and was lost in tumult.

Red Wolf had gone charging up the shallow trickle of water. The current was still troubled; the very spray beaten by the flying hoofs seemed to hang in the sunlight. At a turn, Kenly sighted the quarry, sharply reining about to ascend the bank. With a heave and a lurch, the yellow figure of the girl clutched across his high knees, he sent up his horse, up and through the brush above, again disappearing.

Up went Kenly, but losing time at the scrambling ascent. Up, through the brush, and along the floor of a cañon which mounted to the arid mesa land above. The Comanche, flagged by that glint of yellow, was well in the lead but aware of pursuit. Kenly laughed grimly to himself as he settled down to the work. Were Doña Maria across the other saddle, would he spur so hard? Not likely.

The redskin's pony had the legs of him for the moment; he had expected this. A fast, showy mount, but with no stamina. His own horse was a hard, tough machine of bone and blood which could endure long and far. Content that they were not circling back upon the lost column, Kenly held his mount to a steady gallop.

Dry and arid, the upland appeared as they debouched from the cañon; sandy and stiffly brushed with mesquite. It stretched out far to eastern hills, toward which Red Wolf seemed to be making. Poor ground enough for fast riding, cut up by dry wash and arroyo and thorn.

Turned, rabbit-like, by these deep washes, the Comanche could not leap them with his double burden. He plunged into them, avoided them, doubled and rode like a madman, with skilled bridle; for a little he held well ahead. Kenly dared not take chances of crippling his horse with similar madness. The miles flowed past, foam began to fleck the horses.

On and still on, grimly hanging to the chase. Red Wolf pushed his steed hard, but the ground gave him the disadvantage. An hour passed, and another, before the bent back of the Comanche and the fluttering dress of the girl began to grow more distinct. Josefa lay lax, as though she had fainted. Her white face, her streaming hair, hung down from time to time.

Kenly's restraint, his refusal to accept the challenge to a madder pace, seemed to infuriate Red Wolf, whose bow was gone but not his lance. He lashed on and on with cruel hand. The horizon was clear of any other moving shape; if Red Wolf expected help to come up, he was mistaken. But the eastern and northern hills were closer now.

Not close enough for safety. The pony was flagging visibly.

Foam-flecked, the horse of Kenly had strength left and to spare, and gradually crept up on the other. To the right opened out a deep arroyo. Sighting a broken bank, the Comanche whirled and drove headlong down in a wild scramble to the sanded rocky bottom.

Kenly plunged after, then touched in the spur. Around a turn, and ahead showed the straightaway stretch that he wanted. His spurs drove in, he reached the pistol from its holster and waited. Closer they drew, and closer. The broad back of the Indian offered fair mark; above it the down-crouched head. Josefa hung down across the rider's knees; little enough danger of hitting her.

The distance narrowed. Fifty feet, then forty. Kenly threw up his long weapon, aimed carefully, and pressed the trigger.

EVEN WITH the belch of smoke, the recoil, his horse had slipped on loose rocks, with a falter and a flinch of pain. He clutched frantically on the reins. With one quick, savage yell, the Comanche whisked his animal around, and drove down with lance leveled, with ploughing sand and gravel, with fierce painted face intent.

Kenly was lost and knew it. He braced himself to parry with the pistol—then he saw the lax figure of the girl writhe and uncoil, as the lance came for him. Her arm moved, swung, plucking out the knife from Red Wolf's sheath, driving it in with frantic strength, Kenly sensed the effect rather than the detailed act; his blistered, sweat-blind eyes caught the movement, the flash of steel, the haft nestled against the glistening painted chest.

Down went the lance. The painted visage was caught in a sudden startled spasm; his pony bore him past the American, so close that the sweaty reek of him struck upon Kenly's nostrils. Like a horrid vision of paint and blood he swept by, the girl struggling to free herself from his convulsive grasp, and so was gone around the bend of the arroyo.

Spurs plunged. The horse leaped, and Kenly came upon them

there a moment later. The heaving pony stood with legs apart, head hanging low, the Comanche lying beside him across the broken lance, face upturned. Kenly slid from the saddle to catch Josefa, who was scrambling dazedly from the sand where she had been tumbled.

"You are hurt?" he gasped, dry-throated.

"No, no!" Her wide eyes blazed with warrior fire. "There he is, look at him—ah, how was it ever done? How did I do it?"

She shivered as she stared down. Kenly turned and looked. The Comanche had one hand outflung. Fingers of the other fumbled at the jutting haft that rode his heaving chest. Then the fingers relaxed and slid away.

"*No bueno—maldita—maldita* Doña Maria—" And with that "damned doña" his fierce spirit burst free upon a surge of reddened spume, leaving his hot eyes cold and vacant. The eagle aspect of him remained. In death as in life he was proudly handsome; only, as he lay here after last confession, something cynical grew in his look, as though he had been mocked, and repaid mockery with scorn.

"*Dios!* He is dead—dead. We must go."

The girl's voice, her shiver, wakened Kenly to the situation. She was clinging to him, sobbing hysterically with the reaction. He patted her shoulder, soothing her, holding her for the moment as she yielded gratefully to his arm. The sense of her brave loveliness stirred within him, he felt his pulses hammering; he knew suddenly how that Indian must have felt in looking upon her.

"Wait," he said, unsteadily, and loosened her arms. He went to the pony and reached for its dangling reins of plaited horsehair, brought the two animals together. His own horse stood with one foreleg flexed and trembling. That slip on the loose rock had caused the sprain.

Kenly swiftly rubbed down the two animals. Josefa came to him, pale now, wide-eyed, uncertain; he smiled and took her hand, and swung her up gaily into his own place. He stood laughing up at her, joying in her beauty, until color crept into her cheeks and a smile to her lips.

"My horse for you, the other for me," he said. She started suddenly.

"The knife, the knife! We may need it, *señor*."

Kenly grunted and stooped, stiffly, for he was saddle-sore. By that wet, thong-wrapped haft he plucked the red blade free, and hastily thrust it, unsheathed, through his belt. Then he swung up into the heavy Spanish saddle, the saddle of a chief; the pony obeyed the pressure of the cruel Spanish bit.

The two of them rode slowly down the arroyo.

Red Wolf made no protest; he was done with war and women. He stayed, with the broken lance for symbol of his checked ambitions.

"The horse is lame, *señor*."

"It will carry you," Kenly replied. "We cannot ride fast, but no matter. You saved my life this day, my dear—that lance was due for me."

She looked at him and smiled, and sobered again.

"God sent the time. I had been held too tight before; then God sent the time and gave the arm. Let's not speak of it again, Don Hugo. Where do we go?"

"*Quien sabe?*" and he shrugged. "Climb out of here first, and see."

"What of the others? My mother dead—and Pablo? But she would fight; she can fight like a man, she says."

Kenly shook his head, and lied a little.

"No danger. There were the soldiers and the muleteers. I heard muskets shooting hard, and those Indians don't like close work. No, we'll find them safe."

She brightened a little. The back trail led out of the arroyo. The sun was by this time lower than Kenly had expected.

The broken plain stretched afar, the girl's mount limped ever more pitifully, and there was no trail to follow; and the gray dusk fell.

CHAPTER IX

GRAPE AND BULLETS

THE COLD gloom turned into cheer. Water and trees coming with the last fringe of daylight, and naught else needed. The fire flickered a little. From the saddle pockets, dry packaged meat-strips, hard and tasteless but good enough to serve.

And, like the exterior scene, Kenly's mental confusion slowly passed as they talked. Things came plain enough now, and the old bewilderment died. It started with a smile and a laugh, as she turned to him.

"And if it had been that Doña Maria, that Conchita, would you have given chase so hard?"

"God forbid, *Josefita mia!* He could have carried her to the devil," and Kenly laughed with her. Then she sobered.

"It was the devil's daughter behind all this. She arranged it. I was his pay; I know it now. He told me as we rode. You understand? She hated me. She was jealous of me in that room when Santa Anna looked at me. She didn't like my caring for you. She even laughed at your face. She has no heart, that one!"

"You don't like my face, little one?"

"Bah! You have more to you than that. She has only her face. Yes; she planned it all with the chief. Red Wolf was to take me for his own, his men would kill the rest of you. And so, out of her way."

Kenly shivered a little. The night had thickened, the stars were bright, the air was chill. They had the saddle-blankets for warmth, and the little fire; they had no fuel or courage for a larger blaze.

Clever, this girl! And shrewd. She had not been fooled at all. Kenly drew her closer. She huddled against him, frankly.

"That's better; we'll stay warm, at least. Santa Anna did not know about all this; he would not have given me to the Indian. He had other plans, I think. Well—"

"You are afraid of him? Afraid to go back to Bejar?"

"Yes, and no. But you cannot go back there, Don Hugo," she said earnestly. "You have your own road."

"Whither?" And he laughed harshly. "No, my dear; I'll take you back, at least to within sight of Bejar, if we can find our way, With a lame horse, we've no haste. If we happen on the Texans, well and good; they'll not harm you. Undoubtedly Pablo and the others will have turned back ere this, and you'll find your mother there."

A comforting word and thought for her. Presently she was asleep, her face against his shoulder; and Kenly, wondering at the strangeness of it, passed into slumber himself. Thus the night passed.

The dawn broke fair and clear, although the season of rains was at hand. To their joy, the lameness and swollen fetlock of the horse was relieved; he scarce limped at all beneath the light weight of the girl. They breakfasted on water and the tasteless chips, made the best of things with a laugh, set forth and made good time into the southward.

The years fell from Kenly this day, until he was a boy again, jesting, laughing, as they rode under the southerly sun, that warmed them but did not burn. His face was tanning where the bandages had lain, and it was knitting, gaining strength. He felt more himself.

A joyous day in these empty lands, with never a sign of smoke or of man on any horizon. They were together in a new world, drawn ever closer one to the other, and Kenly marveled at the gay creature who shared this strange joyous new world with him. A tenderness was upon him when he spoke with her, when he looked at her; all his old roughness was swept away, until he wondered at himself no less than at her.

NO TRAIL, no indication of man's presence, all that afternoon, as they pressed steadily and rapidly into the south. With the set of sun they mounted to a long roll of higher ground, seeking water beyond and finding lush trees and a stream awaiting them. Then the girl's arm came up.

"Look!" she cried. "There, more to the east, past those trees—"

Kenly looked and beheld a grayness against the sky. "Smoke!" he exclaimed.

"Many smokes in one; the smokes of all Bejar!" broke out the girl eagerly. "And clouds coming up from the south. It will be raining there, in the country of many rivers, all this night. You shall see. And the cooking fires are burning so that the whole town sends up white smoke, and they are warming the houses against the rain and cold. Come! Come along and think of our own fire! There's wood in plenty—"

And they sent the horses down the long slope toward their place of bivouac.

With the darkness, the ruddy fire drew them close, held them entranced, and their hands trembled as they looked into the flames together. Kenly knew, then; knew without words, yet dared not venture words. He could feel how she was drawn to him, he knew how his heart trembled, like his strong fingers.

"A short ride in the morning, Josefita. Then it must be *adios*. I cannot go into the town, you know. There's no telling what might come up to crop me."

"Yes; you are right, you must leave me." Her lithe, sweet body quivered a little against him, as she sighed. "You must leave me in the morning, let me go on alone to Bejar. I am not afraid. Yes, you must ride fast and far, get rid of this uniform, go among your own people. Or perhaps," and she turned suddenly to look into his face, her eyes eager, "perhaps you will take me with you?"

Madness tugged at him. He would have liked nothing better than to part with all the past save her alone, and by holding fast to the present, shape the future from it.

But they had come too far; the trail had narrowed now. He stifled a groan as he thought of all practical common-sense matters.

"You are safer in Bejar," he said gently. "If you were with me there might be Indians, hardships, the Texans."

"You are not a Tejano, then?"

"Lord forbid!" and he laughed a little bitterly. "They've no love for me, nor I for them. I've naught to do with their quarrels; nor you."

"But you might join them," she exclaimed. "You might fight with them; I will go with you. Don Santiago Bowie will be with them, and he is my friend."

"Not mine," said Kenly grimly. "No; I must strike through Texas and back to my own country. And what waits for me there? Nothing. Less than nothing."

His voice, his heart, his soul, were all gloom and emptiness. The girl nestled closer to him.

"Oh, it is so hard!" she murmured. "It is so hard to understand the world and the ways of it, and why one must do thus, and another so. Pablo is so wise; he has a proverb for everything. But I have not.

"And it seems hard that everything cannot be so lovely and perfect, such as this is tonight—"

Kenly's heart shook. It had come; he knew it, he felt it. He turned his face to her, wordless, and her lips came to his. They sat there for a long space, silent, trembling. Her fingers stirred at last and came to his face and touched it like a caress.

"My dear face!" she said softly, with fluttering breath. "When she, that other one, laughed at it—oh, I could have killed her! I love your face, my Hugo."

"And I you, my heart; yes, I love you, love you," he cried out passionately, desperately, despairingly.

All the frantic truth rushed upon him.

He had nothing, nothing to give her, nothing to offer her; he himself was hunted, harried, hopeless, a man broken and damned. Yet there were worse in the world. He caught her two hands in his.

"Oh, my dear! There are so many things I must do, there is so much I must accomplish—if I promise to come again, can you wait a little for me, with patience?"

Her lips lifted to his.

"What hurts you so, my Hugo? Your voice is terrible. Yes; whether you come, or come not, I shall keep myself for you alone. I swear it," and her words were steady, quiet, lovely to hear in their strength. "There can be no other man in my life, Hugo. I have thought so from the first. But yesterday, today— well, it is the same with you. I can feel it."

"The same," he echoed. "The same. Listen to me, Josefita. I've got something now to fight for, to conquer for."

"To conquer—what? Whom?"

"The devil," he said grimly. "The bad luck that's chased me, scarred me, bit into me. The folly, the roughness, the mad impulse. I've been a fool in many ways.

"Now I'm out to smash it all. I haven't much education, I've no friends—but I've got the strong hand under it all! And the will. That's the big thing; the will."

AND THE stars saw, and perhaps the cold devils laughed as they heard his voice lifting upon the firelight. The will? It was far from him yet, though he knew it not.

Again they slept together this night, hand in hand for warmth and trust and love. With the gray dawn, Kenly loosed from her hand and was up and about, stirring the fire to life, and it was needed. A gray dawn, sunless, with all the sky to the south and east a white dim phantasy.

"Fog!" she cried, seeing it. "It is the mist that comes up from the rivers and the fields, my Hugo—Bejar lies there, indeed!"

"So eager?" he said grimly. She met his eyes and laughed, bravely.

"Eager, yes, for you to go and come again."

His heart warmed to her courage, though it were but the courage of youth.

They rode down and presently the thin mist was around them and on everything. A luminous fog, as though in testament that the sunny future, like the blue sky, was prepared in waiting. Kenly felt a keen exultation gripping him, bred perhaps of daring, perhaps of love and triumph, as he rode with the girl at his stirrup.

The mist brought forth faint distant sounds, tenuous as itself, but indicative of life.

And presently they came into a wagon-track, a road.

"We're not far now," she said, tremulous. "I can find my way onward. Go, ride off before the fog breaks! It will not last long—ah! Ah! What is that?"

The quiet of the blind way was suddenly shattered ahead. A shot, a cannon roar, then volley upon volley of musketry, sustained and long. Through it pierced sharper sounds—the thin, mad crack of rifles, the distant voices of men all together that lifted and died away into more firing.

"Battle!" Kenly's voice shook with excitement. "Fighting!"

"Then you must join the Tejanos!" she cried. "They are taking Bejar—you must join them, we'll join them together!"

If it were battle indeed, then it seemed a battle in the clouds. There were the sounds, but no visible sources. The cannon spoke once again, and twice, no more; the musketry volleyed fainter, the eager crack of rifles rose and rattled louder. Kenly hesitated.

If San Antonio were being taken, this was no time to ride in. If the Mexican troops were out, the dragoons riding down the Texans, this was no time to stop here. If the fields were aswim with grape and bullets in the fog, what to do? One's senses were confused like the medley of confused sounds.

"Whither, Hugo?"

"I don't know," he muttered. "Keep going slowly."

Rifles cracked again. Later, he learned of the picture that fitted the sounds. Ninety of those long rifles, cut off and surrounded in the mist by five hundred of the best Cos could send forth. Ninety of them, cannon crashing upon them, musketry hailing lead upon them, flashing dragoons charging down on them; ninety rifles cracking in the sunrise, blowing death upon the gunners, silencing the musket volleys, smashing the dragoon lines, cutting down the officers—charging the five hundred or what remained of them, and scattering them all to the four winds in gusty exultation and bloody rout.

But only the sounds came lifting upon the thinning fog, as Kenly and the girl beside him headed slowly on toward the city.

A last crack or two, and the rifles died out.

One side or the other, Kenly decided, was beaten. Even as he listened, keyed to seize upon the moment, the sun came thrusting through the mist; as though riven by clamors and golden rays, the fog went drifting in shredded filaments.

Through it lifted and grew San Antonio de Bejar, with its bell-tower of the great church wreathed by eddying wraiths. At the gate were streaming in soldiery, foot and horse in wild confusion, pack mules galloped hither and thither in disarray. Then a quick, stifled cry broke from Josefa, Kenly swung about. Through the mist close upon them appeared dim shapes. They took form. A party of horsemen; the long rifles and broad hats made announcement, but the hail came in Spanish.

"Surrender, you! Don't move—we have you!"

"*Los Tejanos!*" breathed the girl.

The leader came riding in upon them, sure of the rifles behind him. Kenly drew rein. The leader halted with sharp demand.

"Who are you, with this woman?"

From Josefa burst a glad, wild cry of recognition. Kenly sat there, words dying in his throat, a paralysis upon him, his heart failing. A dead man was staring at him; cold blue eyes, masterful visage, ringing voice. He was facing Jim Bowie, living, who had been Jim Bowie, dead.

CHAPTER X

CONFRONTING GENERAL COS

THE OTHER riders had crowded forward. Jim Bowie's relentless gaze touched upon Kenly without recognition, yet attracted by the absolute stupefaction which gripped this apparent Mexican lieutenant. The eyes rested briefly, widened in startled surprise, and an oath snapped forth.

"That knife—here, hand it over! Let's look at it!"

Kenly could not move. Bowie reached forward, seized the knife, and with quick motion jerked it loose, staring at it, cursing softly.

Bowie—alive! Upon the instant, explanation of all mystery flashed through Kenly's brain. What a dupe he had been! Those others must have known it all the while. Santa Anna and Cos had lied to him that they had headquarters. Vengeance of the Veramendi family, indeed—what an absolute lie! Aimed to hold him helpless, aimed to send him to ambush and death.

"Alive!" he croaked, "Alive!"

Bowie caught the words. The blue eyes flickered up, drove at him.

"What's that? By heaven, I believe you're an American! Here, Travis, look at this fellow! Is he the one you told me about?"

Travis, the same met on the road to Goliad, urged his horse forward; sharp-faced as ever, but now with stubby reddish beard. The others, too, caught the words and came edging in, all astare at Kenly. Their voices began to bite.

"American turned Mexican! Look at him!"

"Fighting his own countrymen—give him what we gave the rest of 'em yonder!"

"Rope or bullet, boys, no matter. Let the woman go. Hey, listen, now—"

Travis came close, squinted at Kenly with his mirthless stare.

"Damned funny, Jim; he's changed his face somehow, Not for the better, either. Still, I could swear he's the very one I met up with, the one who had your knife."

"Changed his rig too, and not for the better," Bowie remarked with contempt. "I know his face, somehow; can't place it myself. Look at the knife—tried to wrap the haft and hide it. A clumsy job. Ah—by heaven, where'd he get the knife? I know those eyes of his—he's the man, Travis! The very man! From New Orleans!"

Recognition darkened in Bowie's face. Still Kenly sat, spellbound, wordless. Now Josefa thrust in between them. She knew the tones if not the words, could read the hostile air, the deadly eyes, the swift mutters.

"Don Santiago!" she cried hastily. "You must not be angry. He is Don Hugo Kenly, and he would join the Texans. He is only taking me back to Bejar. You remember me—Josefa Candelaria?"

Bowie looked at her, started slightly, and saw her for the first time. He smiled; with the smile, a sudden change came upon the man. He removed his hat and bowed in the saddle, with the grace, the charm, that captivated all who knew him.

The chestnut hair seemed lighter than Kenly remembered it from that night in New Orleans. Upon the forehead a vivid scar sank back into the hair-roots. Again Kenly saw the hasty stool descending, the fallen man, the dead face upon the floor—

"Ah, Josefa, it is you!" Bowie was saying. "Of course I remember you, my dear little child of dream left wandering from the old days of happiness. But I am sorry to find you with this rascal. He's no friend of yours, surely?"

"But he is, he is, Santiago! He is a good man; you must not

Triumph blazed in his face.

be angry with him. They sent him out to be killed. He may stay with you, and I'll go into Bejar alone."

Bowie straightened in the saddle, and his countenance hardened.

"You're too careless with your friends, *señorita*. This fellow tried to murder me. You see the scar I bear? He's an outlaw, a damned renegade; he struck me down with a foul blow, looted me, and then ran like a coward. Look at the uniform he wears—"

"No, no, Santiago!" cried the girl. "It is impossible; he is not a coward. I tell you he saved me from great danger, and my brother Pablo owes him much, also. He has saved me from the Comanche war chief, El Lobo Rojo. He is a brave man!"

"Red Wolf!"

The name passed around, surprisingly, from mouth to mouth. Bowie's face darkened. He put on his hat again.

"Red Wolf!" cried Travis. "The Mexicans have raised that devil against us—the Comanches are to be loosed on the settlements. Yes, we heard about it—"

"El Lobo Rojo is dead," spoke up the girl, glancing about in wonder. Bowie made a sharp motion.

"Never mind, never mind; I think we're surrounded by a pack of liars everywhere," he said, and his gaze fastened on Kenly. "Well, speak up, you! Is your tongue clipped, like your courage?"

"Yes; by finding that you're alive," said Kenly. "I didn't know you that night, Mr. Bowie. I had no intention of striking you down. There were two men attacking a woman, and I took you for one of the men."

"And took my knife for your own, you would add," Bowie's voice was like steel. "You are a lying scoundrel, sir. You are skulking in Mexican uniform. You're a damned renegade—a traitor to your own blood. You're lower than a rattler, sir! By the Eternal, you gave Jim Bowie a foul blow and—" Bowie checked himself abruptly, but the fierce, fiery blue of his eyes changed not. "Travis, call the boys back a bit, and I'll deal with this hound myself."

"Looks like we done killed enough rattlers this morning," drawled Travis. Then Kenly found tongue, in swift anger.

"You go too far, Bowie," he said. "I'll not be put down by you as a traitor. I thought you dead, killed by my hand unintentionally. I was told you were dead, that vengeance for your death was after me hotfoot, that your friends and family—"

Bowie snarled suddenly at him, like a wolf.

"You heard aright. I'm a dead man. I've no friends, no family; nothing but the cause of liberty. I've no past, no future—bah! You're right, Travis. As for you, you scoundrel, here is the knife. You needn't hide the haft; it's no knife of mine. The blade is foul as your own accursed hand. You're free to go, rejoin your friends, my renegade lieutenant. And this girl—" He paused, glaring again with cold menace. "She's too good a girl to be with you. If she comes to harm by you, look out! Ah—I forgot. You robbed me of more than the knife, that night. The map, eh? That's what you were after all the time."

"That's false," snapped Kenly. "If you want the map, here it is."

HE PRODUCED the folded paper General Cos had given him. Bowie, with a wondering expression, took it and glanced at it. His face changed. He crumpled up the paper with an oath, then thrust it back at Kenly.

"A clumsy forgery, false like yourself. Bah! You're a liar from start to finish. The San Saba silver is not for you or your damned Mexican friends; it's too well covered. Now, clear out!" His voice lifted sharply. "Don't waste powder on this rat, boys! I wish you no harder luck than to stick with your friends, lieutenant. Tell Cos we're coming to call on him. Next time we see you, it's a bullet or rope. Clear out!"

Kenly met the fierce eyes steadily, angrily. Mechanically, he pocketed the map.

"You're hasty, unjust, and in the wrong," he said bitterly. "I can prove to you—"

"Clear out, damn you!"

"Very well. Some day I'll have your apology for this action, these words."

"Some day I'll hang your pelt on the gates of Bejar," rasped Bowie, and turned his back. He gestured to his men and they rode away. Kenly looked after them, trembling with futile anger. Then Josefa touched his arm, timidly.

"What does it mean, Hugo? Did he say that you struck him? Ah, he is terrible in his anger. And the knife—then it was his knife? I do not understand."

"He and all of them will think better of this some day," Kenly said slowly. "Poor devil! No past and no future—"

"It is because of Señora Bowie and the two children, all dead in a day from the cholera," she said. "He is of good heart, my dear; there will come another day, for always God sends the time. And what do we do now? Will you ride away?"

"Small chance," said Kenly. Run for it now, cross Texas, hide himself again in his own country? No, a thousand times no! This called for something else. At the moment, these Texans were in no mood to listen to reason. "We go on to Bejar, my dear."

He sent his horse forward. His bitterness threw everything into a tangle; horns in a bag, as Pablo had once said. He could not blame Bowie, of the hot eyes and the scarred head. That accursed knife! It had served him well and ill again.

"Josefa," he broke out, "you must believe me when I say that the blow was a mistake, and that I did not rob him, but that hag Matilde. She knows, Pablo knows, Don Rodrigo knows. Ask Pablo."

"I believe you, my heart," she said simply. Kenly thrust the knife at her.

"Take it; you've earned it."

"I'll clean it and keep it for Don Santiago," she said. "And you go to Bejar?"

"Yes, by heavens, and I'll have a word with Cos that he'll remember," said Kenly, his voice edged, his eyes stormy and hot with new fury.

So he had been sent to death. Josefa a bribe, Red Wolf bought over to hurl his Comanches on the settlements; all those who knew of the map, wiped out. The map false, the story of the Veramendi family all false—liars, all of them! A score was to be reckoned up, though he himself might come off poorly. The plan had miscarried, but at least he was a lieutenant and an officer, not to be easily silenced. Well, one word more, then! Face down the liar, see what happened, and then go to his own folk and damn the consequences. No more sneaking out of trouble. A new life, a new will, meet the devil halfway from now on! So, his head high, Kenly rode past the sentries at the gates and on into Bejar.

Straight through down to the Alamo, there to report, find General Cos, and have matters out, blast him! Not the town he had left, by a good deal. Wounded men, troops being stationed, powder and shot carried about, barricades being flung up in all the streets. Confusion incident upon the morning's fight was everywhere.

They passed through the town, on across the river, and were dismounting within the Alamo confines, when Kenly heard a glad, eager shout. Pablo came running up, his pocked face in a welter of joy. He caught Josefa in a quick embrace.

"Ah, little one! And it is you, *señor! Gracias a Dios!*"

"My mother, Pablo? And the others?"

Pablo scratched his head, grinning.

"All are back—that is, not all. Your mother's safe. It was only a small affair, my lieutenant. When that accursed chief rode away, his warriors lost heart. We had killed not a few of them, too; those three Americanos fought like devils, I must say. Two of them died, but Mateo and three of the others are still alive. We brought in some scalps, I can tell you! We only got in late last night—"

"Take care of the horses and Josefa," said Kenly abruptly. "Where's General Cos?"

"At the Veramendi mansion, *señor*. You have heard of the battle outside, by the Concepcion mission? Well, you may not see the general; he won't be expecting you."

"Doubtless," Kenly said grimly.

"You see, *señor*, he will be furious. Some one lied to him; I could not make anyone listen to the truth. It is said that you ran away."

"Bah! I'll have a word or two myself, perhaps."

"So may Doña Maria," muttered Pablo. "That damned doña is at the bottom of a good many wells, and it does not pay to fall in—"

A BRUSQUE farewell to Josefa, and Kenly was striding away, back into the town. He was borne, upon a high fury that would devour all obstacles.

Once he paused, and once only, in his course. A small knot

of soldiers and citizens were gawking at a placard nailed upon the front of a closed shop. It was in Spanish and English, hand lettered, proclaiming aloud:

2,000 REWARD FOR THE CAPTURE AND DELIVERY
OF GENERAL COS, TEXAS AND LIBERTY!

A sniff, and Kenly went on.

The audience was hardly won; all headquarters was in wild alarm over the happenings of the morning, and something very like panic was evidenced in places. If ninety men could destroy five hundred, what would the whole army of the Tejanos do when they arrived? Perhaps the artillery would save the day, however.

Kenly was in at last. The big room held aides; General Cos leaned back in his chair at the heavy table. Of all the countenances in the room, his alone was calm; rather, it was controlled by a look of annoyed surprise.

"So, you have returned, sir? You have a report to make, you demand to see me at once. Your business is urgent. Ha! Well, I have small time to waste on failures."

So Cos was resorting to accusation? Kenly, in hot fury, mustered up his Spanish. He flung reserve to the four walls and the winds.

"You be damned. You've already wasted time on failure. Yes, I've a report for you. Lies, a false errand, a false map, a false guide. You stooped low, *señor!* Returned, am I? Not by your doing, not by your hope. You lied to me about Bowie. I met him this morning outside town. He's alive. You traded an innocent girl to that Comanche chief so that he'd lend his help. Well, he's dead and we're not. How do you like my report, sir?"

Ghastly silence around the room, stupefied faces. General Cos sat unruffled, but his color had somewhat darkened. Then he smiled thinly.

"Ah! You met Bowie the rebel—and you live? Good. Perhaps

you returned here of your own free will? Perhaps he sent you to spy upon us?"

Kenly caught his breath with fury. Then the door behind him was flung open. It slammed upon click of rapid heels and swish of angry skirt. Like a blond Jezebel, Doña Maria fronted him.

"You are back! You are here!"

Kenly stared into her eyes coldly. "With the girl you sold into slavery!"

The word sent a tremor upon the room.

"Oh!" Doña Maria whitened. "Captain Flatnose, eh?"

"Silence!" snapped General Cos, and leaned forward with interest in his eyes. "What's this charge about the girl who was here, and the Comanche chief, Maria?"

"You expect truth from her?" flashed out Kenly, and laughed. "She offered the girl to the Indian; where were you in the bargain, that you pretend innocence?"

"*Por Dios!*" exclaimed Cos haughtily. "Do you think that I, a *caballero*—"

"Who sent me to be slain in ambush, and other soldiers with me?"

Doña Maria screamed out. "He accuses me? It is a lie! I tell you—"

"Silence, by the thunders of God! Shut your mouth!" General Cos came to his feet, his calm broken at last. Doña Maria bit her lip. "Lieutenant, I knew nothing of this, I assure you; in fact, His Excellency had other plans for that girl. As for you, what talk is this of ambush? Nothing of the sort. You were given a false map, true; you were sent off on a false trail, true; why? So that you, and the others with you, might run away to follow the map, and the devil swallow you up. If you prate of truth, take it and welcome. And now you are under arrest."

"As you please," said Kenly. "At least I spoke my mind."

"I can forgive boldness," rejoined Cos. "The charge is different. You deserted your command in the face of the enemy. The penalty is the firing squad."

"A false charge, false as the rest," snapped Kenly. "I pursued the Comanche. Red Wolf is dead—a pleasant bone for you, Doña Maria."

"False? That remains to be seen, *señor*. You yourself have admitted meeting the rebel Bowie this morning outside town. We shall look into this. He sent you on in to spy upon us, eh? Well, you can sit in a cell and do your spying," and a smile touched the lips of Cos. "You'll not be a solitary, either. You'll have a guard inside as well as outside. Take him!"

The aides closed in, with a glitter of steel. Kenly was marched away, but his head was high as he departed. At least, he had had his way. He had met the devil halfway, and laughed as they led him out.

CHAPTER XI

THE FACE OF JOSEFA

SILENCE; AND now and again upon the silence, ghostly voices, drifting past the window. Day upon day, sunlight and mist, darkness, mist again and sunlight. Twice a day the door was shoved open, a guard thrust in a wooden bowl and an olla of water, and the door slammed again with rasp of bolts.

How long? Kenly had no idea; he lost track. A touch of fever, for a day or so, threw him off balance. His personal belongings, soap and a razor, such as he had kept on his person; no tobacco, no nothing. Yet he waited in savage patience, a smile in his soul if not on his lips. He had met the devil halfway, at least! The thought lingered. He had far to go, but he had not flinched. The firing squad? Bah! He had doubted that from the first. He had read something else in the eyes of General Cos—something he was far from comprehending. Not the firing squad, however.

Now and again, the distant crack of rifles. Voices outside the window, drifting, floating past and gone again, yet significant.

"They will do nothing, those Tejanos. Our defenders are too strong—"

"They talk, argue, shout, and are afraid to meet us. Their forces are breaking up. Is it true that Santa Anna is bringing up the whole army?"

"*Quien sabe?* Doubtless it is true—"

It was not the calabozo that held Kenly, but an interior room in that very Zambrano Row, cornering upon Acequia and Flores

Streets; that very row past which a private soldier, one Hugo Kenly, had walked guard upon a night now far buried in a maze of circumstance.

The room was of stone walls plastered with mud and thinly whitewashed. Moderate in size, it was lighted and ventilated only by the tiny barred window, too high for reach. The main door was of solid planks armored with iron scrolling and bolt-heads. A smaller door, but similarly fortified, in the side wall, apparently indicated connection with other precincts of the row. It was locked and never opened. For its purpose, the room was well adapted. Kenly was held incommunicado. Yet—there were the voices.

"So the terrible Texans do nothing but camp and argue!" rose a woman's laugh. "And their men drift away—"

"They are like children," barked her escort. "They have no artillery, we have twice as many men as they, the whole town is a fortress—"

Talking, argument, discussion. Kenly could picture the camp outside this barricaded town, with dissension running rife, with politicians and self-seekers playing at soldier, with settlers departing to get in their crops. Rifles against the heavy artillery of General Cos—yes, they were like children, those rough, unruly rebels!

There were no furnishings in the room. A drain in one corner, a pallet of soiled, mildewed blankets, a wooden peg in the wall upon which to hang the olla.

Suddenly, of a morning, there was a rustle and scrape of footsteps, The bolts or bars rasped free of socket, the door was jerked open. A man in shabby private's uniform fairly burst in, staggering under a violent shove. A bundle of bedding was hurled in after him, and the door slammed. The man recovered balance, and with a curse glared about. He was Devore, gaunt, bareheaded, savage.

His baleful eyes fell upon Kenly. His jaw dropped. The

startled expression of his unshaven countenance was ludicrous, although his company was most unwelcome.

"For cripes' sake!" he blurted. "'Tain't you, is it? Well, this *is* a go!"

"No choice of mine," snarled Kenly.

"So that's what they meant?" Devore erupted in a torrent of oaths. "Found me stuck in the wrong jug, they said—thought I was here, huh? And I been cussing for bein' stuck away in that damned calabozo! And now look at me—*arrgh!*"

Kenly caught the words with a flash of understanding. He could interpret now the parting jollity of General Cos. Devore was to have been his cell mate, and somebody had erred. Kenly laughed harshly. Devore stared at him.

"Last I seen of you, you were streakin' it, leaving me and the rest up a tree with them Injuns. By the looks of your back, I thought none of us would ever see your ugly mug again. So Cos jugged yuh, huh?"

"You blasted scoundrel!" said Kenly angrily. "You're the one who reported me deserting, huh?"

"Had a good reason, didn't I?" Devore replied sulkily. He picked up his bedding and kicked it into pallet shape along the unoccupied wall.

"You knew good and well I took after that Comanche guide of ours."

"Yeah!" and Devore jeered at him, then produced a twist of tobacco and bit at it. He mouthed the chew for a moment, and continued. "Yah! With that map o' the San Saba country in your pocket, huh? Oh, I heard all that yarn ye told about fetching the gal in and so forth—but I don't swaller that for a minute."

Kenly laughed. "Better get your swallowing apparatus in shape, then. Yes, I fetched her back and then had to come into the city. Couldn't help myself."

"You're slick, all right. I heard you'd damned the gin'ral to his face, too. But what game were you and that Injun chief up to, huh? Where's he now?"

"Wolf meat." Kenly's ire rose at this confident braggart who refused to believe the obvious truth, thinking himself so smart. Devore was more than braggart, he knew; apt at any deviltry.

"What? You done for him?"

"Somebody did, at all events."

"Why, you cussed fool! When he knowed where that Almagres silver is, and all he wanted was the gal? And you let that chance slip, when you might have palavered with him—oh, hell!" Devore spat disgustedly, then mused darkly. "You come with the gal—how'd you git through them Texans?"

"They passed me through, both of us."

"Huh! On account of the gal, and not knowing you with that face, sure. Hey! Didn't happen to meet a particular friend of yours out there, did ye?" and Devore grinned.

"So you know Bowie's alive, do you?"

"HELL, YES; I've knowed it all along," and Devore chuckled. "I knowed he wasn't dead that night in New Orleans, anyhow up to time we made the schooner, And 'cause why? I was back at the Beausejour for licker after you thought you'd laid him cold, that's why. They said it'd be nip an' tuck with him; but he's the kind hard to kill. I had no call to set you easy about him, blast you! So you seen him out there, huh?"

"Yes," said Kenly shortly.

"And he let you go—didn't know you, huh? Well, you've got me to thank for that face, mister."

"Damn your impertinence, I've got you to thank for nothing," Kenly snapped. Devore rolled his quid, eyed him with calculation, and grinned again.

"Lookit, now. You cracked Bowie's head and made your getaway with us. You'd be a damn sight better off if he was dead; he don't forget a blow. You ain't out of the woods by a long shot—once he knows what you look like now. Remember that," and the man surveyed Kenly with bloodshot eyes, low cunning in his brutal features. "You're too high-faluting to take up with the likes o' me, huh? Well, think ag'in, mister. It's you and me together.

"We're the only white men in Bejar who know about that San Saba business and where the mines lay. That's why Cos has put us here."

"How about your two cronies?"

"Them?" Devore named his two companions from New Orleans, with an oath. "They're back yonder with their hair lifted. After you lit out, the three of us made a break, figgering to follow you; but them Injuns done for the other two. I slipped back into camp. Damned if they didn't put up a fight, women and all! We just did get here 'fore them damned Texans showed up, too."

"And you reported me to Cos, you lying devil!"

"Well, why not? You shot me, didn't you?" said Devore impudently. "This leg still bothers me like hell, and you come off with a new face and another purty gal. And it was me give 'em both to you, remember. Yes, I informed on you, and Cos sent for me, and what'd I get, blast him? The calabozo! All for telling him I knowed what was up and I'd do the San Saba job if he'd supply me another outfit, and make me a lieutenant. I told him you'd not be back, not with Jim Bowie in the landscape; and for why. Then he clapped me in the jug—and here I be." Devore spanked his hip with jubilant hand. "Luck, I call it."

"The luck's all yours," Kenly said dryly.

"No, it ain't." Devore assumed a more friendly air. "You still got the map safe?"

"Yes." Kenly was about to add that it was false, then checked himself.

"Well, it's you and me, mister. S'pose them Texans take the town—it ain't likely, but s'pose they do?

"I'll keep mum on you. You keep mum on me; they got some

regular army men with 'em. Two of us—we'll light out for the San Saba. Suit you?"

"You're wasting breath," Kenly said in contempt. "I wouldn't trust you with the coppers on a dead man's eyes. You can't hold Bowie over me, or the Texans either."

"All right, all right, then I won't," Devore said. "We'll git out of here; then you'll find I'm a right good feller. There's a door that opens; likely only one guard—say, how long you in for?"

"Until they shoot me."

"What's that? Shoot you?" Devore exclaimed in alarm. Kenly shot an oath at him.

"You lying hound, none of your pretending! You told Cos I deserted; and he said it meant a firing squad for me—"

He broke off. Into the staring face of Devore rushed a crimson tide. He shook his fist in the air and his voice broke into a hoarse shout.

"It can't be! I'll tell him it wasn't so! You be shot—and leave me alone, and without that there map? You hand it over! I'm a-going to have it."

"You sure have that map on the brain!" said Kenly. "Keep away from me or I'll drop you in your tracks, you fool."

THAT DEVORE was completely obsessed by the thought of the map and the San Saba silver, was obvious. Indeed, at this moment he looked close to being a madman. He was all in a flurry of greedy inflated fears, embittered hopes, wild chagrin and wilder resolve—his ignorance of this country, his very ignorance in general, made him a prey to chaotic imagination and credulity run riot.

No doubt he thought the silver lay about on the ground for the picking up. He hesitated, fingers clenched to rough palms, his lips atremble. Sweat beaded his flushed features. His haggard eyes measured Kenly with hot insistence.

"I know all the tricks of hidin' a bit o' paper," he growled. "If I have to search you for it, I'll have that map!"

"You lay a filthy finger on me and I'll smash your cursed face flatter'n mine," snarled Kenly. "The map's no good."

"That's a lie." Devore relaxed; those hard, undeviating brown eyes broke him with their steadiness, their animosity. He sank down on his pallet, and a low growl broke from him. "I'm goin' to have that map afore you're took out of here. Mind you." For a space he relapsed into brooding silence, leaning forward to spit, then fastening his eyes on Kenly again.

"I will if I have to throttle it out of you," he muttered, as though to himself. "Cos told me I could have it if I got it. Pumping questions at me like I was a dog! And then puttin' me in here—" the grumbling, throaty voice fell into silence.

Kenly sat in silence, his brain jerking to the words. "Cos told me I could have it!" So Cos had been questioning Devore, eh?

Still something behind all this, still something dark, un-guessed, sinister. Why not shoot these two Americans out of hand and be done with them?

The map, the map! Why had Cos condescended to talk about it with this despised recruit? Kenly's viewpoint cleared a trifle. Devore had bawled out that he would reverse his testimony rather than lose his chance at the map. The man was abso-lutely mad about it. Bowie had not wanted it, Cos had not asked for it, Kenly himself was sick of the thing, whether false map or true map.

Kenly put his head in his hands and tried to think it out. Cos, he felt certain, cared nothing about killing him. That threat of espionage was merely a charge to be held in reserve. Cos had something in him of the hidalgo, of the grand gentleman. He had been outraged, utterly furious, at the exposure of Doña Maria's deviltry. Ah! Doña Maria!

Something seemed to click. Mental transference, perhaps, of sheer desperate thought.

Devore relapsed again, into his dull stare, his mumble. Kenly sat in thought. A glimmer of light had reached him, but only a glimmer.

Heels clicked in the street. A ghostly voice floated in. A thin, ghostly voice indeed, like a loud whisper.

"*Señor!* Can you hear me, *señor*, is that your window?"

Kenly lifted himself—rather, was lifted by that voice in rapid Spanish. Pablo, honest Pablo! He glanced at Devore, who was sunk in glowering mood, had heard nothing or had not distinguished the words. Kenly, beneath the window, straightened up, stretched, yawned with exaggerated tone.

"Ho, ho-ho! Yes. Speak on."

"All is well," came the swift-winged ghostly voice. "The rooster loves the cockerel who crows bravely. Fear not. He admires you. A friend is at hand also—" The voice trailed off into lilting song and went drifting away on the sunlight. Kenly came back to his pallet again.

Oh, marvel! A very answer to his thoughts, to his wanderings. So. Cos admired him for his bold defiance, his torrent of hot speech! Admiration caused this cell, then? Well, perhaps. Queer things were going on in this town, this center of all Mexican force in Texas—who ruled San Antonio de Bejar, ruled all Texas. Singular human motives were in play. Doña Maria cast aside like an old glove? There was murder in this doing. Yes, Cos would resent what she had done.

A friend at hand? That might mean anything. Kenly sank back into bitterness. Friends? He had no friends. He was alone; darker and ever darker, with no dawn in sight anywhere. Darkest before dawn? He jeered mentally at the phrase.

KENLY SAW himself committed to hard quarters, with this fellow glowering across the room. Devore sat hunched and brooding, maundering to himself, darting malevolent bloodshot glances; the obsession of the map, his wild imaginings, had taken full hold upon him. Crazed, perhaps, with the easy white tequila, so easily obtained; a fiery liquor that brought madness to the brain.

So the long day slipped past the grated opening, and while heels clicked and voices floated past, the voice of Pablo Saccaplata came no more. By the gradual rising shadows it was getting on to day's end.

Devore had subsided into an uneasy doze, flat and sprawled, then slept profoundly but with the twitchings and mutterings of troubled dreams. At last he wakened, started up, stood staring around, tousled of thatch and red-rimmed of eye.

"What's this?" he cried hoarsely. "I thought them Texans were on us and set to hang me. I won't be ketched, I tell you! They've sworn to shoot any of us caught in Mexican uniform. I'm getting out, hear me? Hello, there, mister. I guess I was dreaming, huh? Did you hear Santy Anny is coming back?"

"No," Kenly replied. "Is it true?"

"I dunno. Bringing the hull army, they say. Slow business, though; weeks and months—hey!" Devore started in sudden recollection. "Remember, I aim to have that there map afore you're took out—"

The map! Let the obsessed fool have it then; but no. Kenly eyed Devore grimly. Give in to this madman? Never.

There was a grating at the door. The bowl of mush, with two wooden spoons sticking in it now, was thrust inside; an olla of water; the door slammed again. With animal growl Devore sprang forward. Kenly was just in time to stand defense of the rations, and perhaps of himself. He stood over the bowl, fists clenched.

"What'll it be? Spoon, for spoon, with you keeping your distance?"

"All right, all right," whined Devore. "I'm famished; it's share and share alike, ain't it? All right, then. If you go to grab—"

"Sit down."

With the bowl between them, they spooned at arm's length, eyes upon each other. Kenly had the situation in hand, but he found himself dreading the night. Having gobbled until the spoons scraped bottom, Devore lurched back to his pallet. Kenly returned to his own couch, warily taking the bowl with him.

Darkness drew down, the cold night mist; Kenly shivered

under the thin covering. The raucous breathing of Devore passed into a regular undeviating snore. Blinking into the darkness, Kenly found the heavy, regularly punctuated silence weighing down his lids. His eyes insisted upon rest, while outpost ears served sentry duty.

He waked with a start, eyes wide, every sense keen. What had roused him? All was silence—ah! The very silence, the sudden cessation of guttural sound. The cold hand of close and stealthy dagger set his heart to pounding furiously, his flesh to crawling.

"Damn it!" he muttered. "I'm a fool."

His own voice startled him, relaxed his tension. A fluttering sigh from across the room, a grunt, a shift of position; the heavy breathing began again, regular and unchanging, softly sliding into a snore. A fool indeed. The fellow over there was sawing wood for all he was worth.

Kenly sank back. For a space his fingers, his feet, held tension; while this lasted, he could not sleep, he knew. Sleep! Nonsense; he must sleep, Devore would not dare attempt anything. Slumber would have brought sanity to his obsessed brain.

Yet the darkness felt charged with evil. For a stolen moment, as he fancied, Kenly drowsed away again; and suddenly, the monitory hand again plucked at his senses. With a wrench, he burst wide awake, aquiver with suspense. How long had he slept? The room was deathly, mysteriously silent. He could hear nothing, he could see nothing, but a prickling at his nerve-ends brought sweat to his face.

Pent breath, sly and cautious movement stealing athwart the black silence. Then, as Kenly lay rigid and strained, every faculty intent, he did hear. Stealthy movement broke the spell. Up he sat abruptly, and challenged with a voice torn from tight throat.

"Devore? What are you up to, damn you?"

No answer. Slow movement receding now. Then a rustle of the blankets, a muttered groan, a craftily feigned wakening.

"Hey! Wha's matter?"

"None of your tricks. I heard you. Keep your own side of the room."

"You be damned. Save your gab till daylight and lemme sleep."

Sleep he did, by the signs. Kenly fought slumber; this time he had not deceived himself. He must stay awake. That cautious movement peopled the darkness with horror and wild imaginings. Stay awake, yes; but it could not go on for ever. There was a mad maggot in the brain yonder. Better, perhaps, let the fellow have the map of his crazed desire—Kenly yielded, insensibly.

A DREAM rushed upon him; the claws of a nightmare fiend were clutching at his throat, sinking into his flesh, throttling him. Dreams, filled with combat, with creeping things—but it was no stark illusion that sprung him awake. The early gray of dawn. Fingers of flesh and bone fumbling at him. As his eyes opened, the avid visage of Devore was drenching him with hot and eager breath.

A gasp of realization. With frantic revulsion he flung the beast from him; as he came to his feet, Devore grappled him, snarling oaths. Kenly's fist smashed in, again and again; the blows were unfelt, ignored. Devore had amazing strength. Like a wild beast indeed, he sought to pull down, to throttle, to tear.

Kenly twisted suddenly, got the gnashing, snarling head thrust back under his elbow, thrust knee to stomach; a wrench and a heave, foul breath hissing in his face, and a sudden scream burst from Devore. He crumpled, was broken loose, was sent in a headlong sprawl on his pallet.

"You've done for my leg ag'in! Oh, damn your blasted soul, my leg, my leg!"

"I'll do for you as well as your leg, next time," panted Kenly, and dropped back upon his own rags.

The scuffle, the curses, the scream of Devore, brought no query from the outer world. Evidently the guard took no heed what the two Yanquis might do or say.

Wet and heaving, Kenly strove to steady his nerves. He lay

watching the brightening gray of daylight; despite his efforts at composure, he was fagged physically and mentally. His brief periods of sleep had brought no rest; his inner consciousness, his muscles, his brain itself, had been on the alert.

Evidently Devore had suffered no great injury. He sat up presently, and his voice came in a growl.

"I aim to have that map off'n you yet, blast you! And once I get it, by the 'tarnal I'll know what to do with it." The growl subsided into a rumble of self talk. "Make everything hunky-dory for me, that's what. Bowie'll pay to have that map back. Take me in and ask no questions—"

Kenly whistled softly to himself. So here was sense at last! No madness after all. Devore was ridden by fear of his past. If he fell into Texan hands, he counted on that map to save him from any army officers who might know him. The poor devil was obsessed with the value of the map—thought that Bowie would pay for it!

The door was opened. The guard thrust in the olla and a cracked wooden bowl.

"Come, *hombres!* The other bowl!" he directed. Kenly caught up the supper bowl to hand him. Through the air came a dull, heavy report.

"What's that? Cannon?" asked Kenly.

"Cannon, yes." The guard grinned. He was a young fellow, amiable enough. "Those Tejanos are breaking camp and departing. The general is hastening them with one of the big guns from the Alamo. *Hasta luego!*"

It was the first time Kenly had exchanged any word with his guards. A flutter of gay voices, of laughter, of distant cheering, came in upon the window. Devore hitched himself around to grab his share from the bowl Kenly put down.

"What'd he say, mister?" he demanded as he scooped up a spoonful of mush. "Was that fighting—listen! Another cannon. Eighteen pounder, by cripes!"

Kenly grinned at him and was prompted to malicious report.

"Yes; he said the Texans are attacking. Prob'ly they'll be in the town before nightfall."

Wild alarm leaped in the gaunt countenance of Devore. He ate hurriedly, his breath coming in quick gasps, his animal courage sapped by mortal fear. He gobbled down his food and hitched himself back on his bedding.

"I won't have it!" he broke out. "We're shut in here. We're liable to be ketched. I won't have it—I tell you, I won't be ketched like a rat and strung up or shot! I'll fight 'em—gimme a chance, gimme a chance!"

He leaped up, hurled himself at the door, battered it furiously and vainly; and fell back again, sobbing with spent strength, sucking his bleeding hands, glowering and muttering.

"Ketched like a rat in this Mexican uniform!" came his voice in panic. "If the town's took we'll starve to death in this hole afore we're found! And if we're found, by cripes, it's the firing squad—"

AFTER A time the man fell asleep. Kenly did not regret his lie; at least, it had served to twist Devore's mind away from him.

The cannon sounded no more. The daylight hours wore on, Kenly dozed a little, envying the deep and profound slumber which held Devore fast bound; He himself dared not sleep.

Late in the afternoon Devore wakened. He stirred, sat up; became restive as the wolf which, having kenneled for the day; looks forward to the night call.

"They ain't took the town yet," he muttered, listening. "Night's the time. That's when they'll bust in. I got to have that map. I got to git out o' here—"

His maunderings fell quiet; he bit at his twist of tobacco and chewed steadily.

The afternoon light thinned and paled. There came a rasp of bolts at the door; it swung outward to disclose the shadowed figure of the guard, bowl in one hand, musket in the other, face gloomed by the long visor of his cap. He started forward to put down the bowl.

"So you want the other one—then take it, damn you!"

The snarl burst from Devore. Like a dog unleashed on the quarry, he caught up the empty bowl in mid swoop, uncoiled from his pallet, and with a leap brought down the bowl upon the guard's high-capped crown.

Already cracked, the wooden bowl flew in fragments. Cap driven over eyes, the soldier pitched forward. Almost before his musket clattered on the stones, Devore had swept it up. He faced about with the weapon at charge, bayonet flickering.

"Out wi' the map, damn you!"

His unshaven face was a quivering mask of fury. No wavering now in those bloodshot eyes, no least indecision in that gaunt countenance. His soldier training showed in his poise; no mercy in those blazing eyes.

"The map, I say!" lifted his voice. "Hand it over!"

The body of the guard, face down, lay as the only barrier between them. The dusking room was very still; Kenly's gaze held that of Devore for the instant.

"All right," he said quietly, and produced the folded bit of paper.

"Drop it and stand back!" snapped Devore.

Kenly obeyed. The paper eddied to the floor, and it fell near Devore. He stooped warily, eyes and musket vigilant. He groped for it, found it, dared a glance at it, and tucked it away. Again he stooped and groped, found the guard's cap, yanked it free, put it on his own head.

He backed to the open doorway, his musket at cock, blazing triumph in his face. Then he was outside, slammed the door to, and was gone.

Kenly started forward. Freedom beckoned; out of this, off to join the Texans! A sense of shock checked him, as his eyes flitted to the figure on the floor. A tumble of glossy hair had appeared there. Kenly knelt swiftly, turned the body of the guard over. Long black hair framed a face—the face of Josefa.

THERE WAS no blood. The bowl had shattered easily; much of the blow had been spent upon the cap and the coiled mass of hair. Josefa's face was white, colored only by the stain of her parted lips and the dark lines of curved brows and drooped lashes.

Kenly forgot all else, forgot Devore, freedom awaiting. He lifted the girl and laid her on his own pallet. He was about to bring water from the olla when she sighed, and her eyes fluttered open.

"Josefa! You're all right? You know me?"

In the fading reflection of the twilight her arms crept up about him.

"Ah, Hugo!" After a minute she sat up, unaided. "I remember—there was someone else in here. A beast's voice, a strike—"

"It was the other American. The man Mateo."

"But he struck me—he struck me!" Her eyes drove about the room.

"He thought you a soldier, my dear; he's gone, took the musket and ran for it." Kenly pressed her hands; her eyes came back to him in reassurance, in soft warm greeting.

"It's been so long, my dear, so long!" she said gently. "I could not come before. We had to await the day—God sends the time, always. The right man on guard—"

"Why are you here?" burst out Kenly. "My dear, this is insan-

ity! It might have got you into trouble everywhere. Unless there
was a reason."

"A better reason than seeing you again?" She smiled suddenly at him, drew back her arms, began to stow up her loosened
hair. A swift flood of eagerness, of avid happiness, came into
her face.

"Well, there's a reason, true. I came for you, Hugo; we'll go
together. As soon as darkness falls. Don Santiago will be
waiting—Don Santiago, you comprehend? Pablo arranged it
here for me, I arranged it there for you—"

"Bowie?" The word broke from Kenly. "You don't mean
Bowie?"

"But yes. Listen, my Hugo; I went out to their camp, I saw
Don Santiago. Ah, what a *caballero!* He is all iron and fire, that
man. I talked with Pablo and straightened everything out in
my own mind, first; I learned everything. I laid it all before Don
Santiago—that you are a good man, you had been deceived,
you are not a soldier for Mexico but would fight for Texas. I
asked Don Santiago to take back his knife, and you with it.
Hugo, he believed me—almost! And he will believe you and
me if we do something—well, that is all cleared up. That was
my work there."

She was all aglow, all delicious eagerness, Kenly listened in
stupefaction.

"Bowie will listen to reason, then! That's glorious, Josefita—"

"But wait, wait!" She thrust him aside, laughing. "Pablo has
been at work here for you. General Cos knows now that you
did not run away, that you only chased El Lobo Rojo to save
me. He admires you. He has kept you here to keep you safe
until word came from *El Presidente* about you."

Bewilderment here, even though it verified already sent information. She caught at his arm.

"Tonight, Hugo! I have arranged everything with Don Santiago. In half an hour from now, when it gets dark, General Cos
is going to inspect a new battery placed between the town and

the Alamo. Don Santiago and some of his men will be hiding there along the creek. You are to be there—I have a cap for you, a cloak. Don Santiago trusts you to join the escort and carry off the general when the rifles begin to speak. Pablo has a horse waiting for you. It is desperate, but it will be a surprise, and Don Santiago says you're the man for it if you want to join the Texans—"

Fantastic? Kenly suddenly perceived the actual possibility of the harebrained project, as it first appeared. It could be done readily, under cover of the falling darkness. Uniformed already, with cap and cloak, on horseback, he could fall in with the general's escort. Bowie's riflemen would open up unexpectedly. To seize Cos and get away with him—horse and spurs! Not only feasible, but it would work. And he was the man for it. Well said!

"Good! Good!" breathed Kenly eagerly. "But you, Josefa?"

"We will go now. There are no guards outside. The man here was a friend of Pablo, who arranged it. I will steal away to the camp of the Texans. Come, we had best be gone—I will give you the cap and cloak, lead you to where Pablo waits with the horse—"

She sprang up happily. Kenly gave her a hand; the whole thing was flaring in his brain now. With Cos went Bejar! Yes, he was the man for it—

"Ah!" The girl was fumbling at the door now, beating at it. A piteous little cry escaped her. "Help me—it is stuck fast—" Kenly flung himself at the door. Stuck fast, slammed by Devore in violent exit? Fast it was, but not stuck; It yielded to his thrusting only by the slight play of the socketed bolts.

"Locked!" cried out Josefa, aghast. "He did it, that other man—"

Yes. Devore had done this, deliberately, vindictively. There was a terrible silence; then, like a caged bird, Josefa went fluttering to the other door in the side wall, trying it, beating at it, falling back from it.

"That one's always locked," said Kenly. Dull reaction was upon him. But she fired up swiftly and darted to him.

"Here! I have the knife, Hugo. You and I, the knife and the general, all to Don Santiago—there is still time! I think God willed me to bring the knife." She snatched it from under her loose uniform tunic. It was clean again. In the dusk the heavy blade glinted; the silver work of the haft, bared now of bloody wrappings, palely glimmered. "Cut with it, dear one! Quickly!"

A chance, at least. Kenly seized the blade.

HE TRIED one door, then the other. The iron scrolls and studs clinked to the nibbling point; they had been masterfully designed. The stingy intervals of wood did not admit the broadness of the blade. The wood itself was hard-seasoned, the stone jambs were flinty.

In the uncertain light, with eyes straining and grip sweaty, Kenly grimly pecked and slashed and drilled, until weary hands and blade and door agreed: Enough!

"No use." Panting, he stepped back in despair, and his arm fell. "Scarcely could an axe break through this ironbound wood. Useless. Here; take the knife. Keep it."

"We have failed!" she breathed. "Don Santiago will not understand—"

A sob burst from her; she leaned against him, in a moment she was gathered sobbing in his arms. Words were useless.

Still holding her, he sank down upon the pallet, trying to comfort her. The brave spirit of her, housed in that slender frame covered by private's uniform, was broken by this ghastly stroke of fate.

They fell upon silence, huddling there. Darkness had settled down. From without came silence of the night, complete brooding stillness, the air heavy with gathering rain. Sound carried far upon such atmosphere. Kenly's head lifted suddenly.

He caught a sound lifting across the silence. A faint, thin, distant sound that missed the girl's ear completely. It was like nothing he had ever heard except perhaps the scream of a trapped and burning horse. Yet it came from man's throat, somewhere afar in the night, followed by a short, savage lilt of shouted words he could not distinguish.

Yet others caught them and thrilled to that blare of sound bursting from the very soul of a man. A shout, and words, destined to echo across long years.

Others, not so far away as distance went—just up the creek where the Texans were spraddled and sprawled in makeshift camp. The order had gone forth, for General Austin was hopeless of daring anything. Days of rain and wet powder, ragged men, no supplies, no reinforcements.

A few hundred frontiersmen and settlers gathered here in sorry army, disputing, bickering, intriguing. The men, not a third enough to face the ranks of General Cos, already breaking away, the ranks melting daily. Complete absence of all discipline. Nothing but rifles and scant powder with which to face heavy artillery, grape, barricaded streets and houses, the fortress of the Alamo and superior forces—no wonder Austin gave up.

Retreat. Give up the hope of taking Bejar, Retreat and negotiate. Then it was that the heart-flurried scream of sheer frenzied agony burst from a man, and to a barrel-head by the fire leaped the man himself. All knew him. Ben Milam, insurgent and rebel, frontier fighter, legislator, officer in three armies—Ben Milam, who had come alone and hungry through six hundred miles of desert to fight for Texas.

"Retreat!" murmured his voice. "Retreat! Quit cold! Be damned if I do." And then the shout lifted, the words that carried like a trumpet-blare through the hungry, discouraged, failing ranks, the cry that overthrew all authority and changed the eddying current of history in this tiny corner of the world.

"*Who'll go into Bejar with old Ben Milam?*"

To Kenly, crouching in the darkness of his cell, came succeeding silence; and then a clamoring outburst of men's voices that swelled upon the night and died again. What it all meant, if it meant anything, he knew not. Yet he thrilled to the savage quality of that sound; the sheer eerie vibrance of it sent his spine a-tingle.

SILENCE AGAIN, and despondency that gripped him. Lower, ever lower; when the lowest point was reached, another yet farther down appeared, Bowie and those others must have awaited him in vain, thought him surely traitor now. All the girl's work in vain. All Pablo's risk in vain. What devil of a curse lay upon him? He gritted his teeth in the darkness. Win! He would win despite all the devils!

Josefa had fallen into slumber. So pitifully frail and lovely! He gently lowered her upon the blankets, stirred stiffly aside, covered her over. What the devil would be the outcome of all this? The regular sentry must return soon. At least he would let the girl out; he was not unfriendly. At thought of Devore, Kenly's fists clenched.

Suddenly he swung around, incredulous. Yes, it came again. Not from the entrance, but from the other, the hitherto closed door. A rasping scrape of bolts, penetrating thinly. Then the door swung; the prison room flickered to the smoky flare of a torch held above the threshold.

Kenly blinked, astounded, at a group of faces there. A background of swarthy men, the torch-holder and other privates. In the opening an officer. And the foremost figure, cloaked and hooded, yet still brightly gleaming—Doña Maria. And to his utter astonishment, her first words were fair, friendly, as Kenly involuntarily lurched forward to hide with his body the room's secret.

"Come, my Hugo—you are free! The general wishes no more of you; so off you go to the Tejanos, who are breaking camp and marching off. As for that other, in here with you, he stays. Come along!"

Kenly came closer to her, scowling, doubting. The room wavered with shadows. His own shadow and that of the doorway obscured the pallet where Josefa lay; thank heaven the torch had produced him first to sight!

"What's all this?" he demanded. "Some trick of yours?"

Doña Maria stamped her foot; but her smile was radiant, dazzling.

"No, no! See, I am come to make amends to you for everything, Hugo. You are to leave Bejar; you can do less harm outside than in. Come along, then!"

What to believe? Josefa had not stirred; Kenly's brain raced on the thought. He must go, leave her undiscovered—she would be released by the guard. He must go, before this she-devil knew the girl's presence.

He stepped on, across the threshold. At this, the torch must have cast a wider flare into the room.

"*Santo Dios!* That—look there—it is she, the little hussy! It is she!"

The voice of Doña Maria choked upon surging passion. In brief silence, punctuated by her rapid breathing, by the ribald murmurs of her escort, Josefa sat up, rose, stood there blinking at them all. Then again rose the tones of Doña Maria, now sharpened upon a high, shrill note of rage.

"Ah, you are indeed a *soldadera*, a camp follower—here with your man, eh? A husband for you, said *El Presidente*, ha, one is found already—"

Kenly whirled on her. "Damn you, keep your tongue off her! She is—"

"Silence him, Leon."

Kenly was seized. Briefly, before he could struggle, hands gripped his arms, a muzzle of a pistol touched his cheek.

"However you got in here—here you stay," went on Doña Maria. "One of you, try that other door. Locked? Right. Look, they have been whittling at it—ha! Try to break these doors, hussy, all you wish! Where's the other man? Gone? Look into all this, Leon. Well, hussy? Have you anything to say?"

Josefa looked at her calmly, and her calm words went deep.

"You are too low for me to see, woman."

"So?" Doña Maria checked impulsive movement and smiled thinly. "You see Don Hugo departing with me, little one. He has come to a good friend now, one who can help him, and who is making ready a great future for him. Sleep well, my *sol-dadera*—"

Kenly broke into sudden convulsive movement. By dint of foot and fist he almost won free to spring back into the room. But he was hedged about by bodies, grappling hands pinioned him against the wall, force of sheer weight held him helpless while the door was slammed and the bolts shot home. Josefa was left to the darkness.

Kenly yielded to pressure, ceased to resist, let himself be shoved along down a hall. This hall opened into the night of the outer air. The torch was extinguished. A heavy, misty night with brooding rain again in the air.

The guarding hands fell away. At a word from the officer, Leon, the men drew back, rimming the darkness, but beyond earshot. Kenly found himself alone with the officer and Doña Maria, who spoke low but vehemently, her hand at his arm.

"Come, my Hugo; no pretense between us. Let us cast off the cloak, eh? You do not love me; but Leon, here, does love me. We have need of you. You want the girl in there? Good; you shall have her as your price."

"Still selling her, are you?" Kenly's voice was hard as steel.

"Bah! This is to your own good and hers. It is you and I and Leon this night. You must reach the Texans before they have all marched away. Tell them that at dawn General Cos is marching out to scatter what remains of them. But first, at midnight tonight, after the ball that is taking place in the Veramendi house, he goes out with his staff to the Alamo. You comprehend? At midnight. And I—I hate him! And Leon hates him."

She hurried on, suppressed fury in her voice. No acting now.

"Tell those Texans to come down and hide among the trees where the road to the Alamo crosses it. You will find them out at the old mill, on the river; easy to find. Tell them he will be with his staff, no one else. There is no danger, you comprehend. They can easily take him and the others. When they have him, they have Bejar; you'll be free man here, the girl will be yours—you see? Forgive me for all the past, my Hugo. The future is born anew tonight, at midnight."

ASTONISHMENT SWEPT Kenly, and suspicion; yet he could feel in his heart that she spoke the truth now, if ever.

The three of them stood close against the entrance. At one side a lantern burned hanging on a hook in the wall. Unseen at first, its gleam had crept gradually upon them. One could see a little now.

Kenly felt the spell of her personality upon him. Traitress? Yes; but the Texan camp beckoned. Queer that she, and Josefa before her, should have picked on the same spot! Yet this plan was by far the better, as Kenly saw instantly. The Alamo was almost part of the city. The Texans were breaking camp, disbanding. Cos would never dream of any danger. No question now of Kenly seizing him—but of rifles speaking from the midnight darkness, of men leaping forth, of assault and death. And she, the traitress—well, that was not his affair. He quivered to the swift urge of it all. Cos had flung her aside like an old glove, eh? And this would be her answer. For Texas!

Yet suspicion still jogged him somehow. He glanced at the officer, Leon. A most urbane fellow, this, sleekly dark, silent, a faint smile touching his lips; a smile, courteous but equivocal, twitching beneath the black mustache.

"Suppose," said Kenly, "that Bowie or the others won't trust me?"

"But they will." Her voice was urgent, persuasive. "He, or any of the leaders, need only be there with their men; they will see. It is your chance to make peace with them, Hugo. And for me, revenge upon him; ah, how he has treated me!" She trembled with a rush of passion. "For you, the girl yonder, kept safe. I dared not let her suspect anything; it is just the three of us. And for Leon—myself. The two thousand pesos that the Tejanos have offered for General Cos? Keep them. Yours, Don Hugo. Yes?"

"Of course," said Kenly.

He saw the officer, Leon, lift hand to mustache, turn slightly in the light, as though this were some signal. Doña Maria swung around, laughing.

"Leon! You will take the *señor* through town, pass him through the sentries?"

"But yes, assuredly," returned Leon, in silky voice. "Just one little formality first, *mi querida*. We must see General Cos."

"What!"

The word burst from her. Then, for a brief instant, she devoured Leon with her blazing eyes, comprehended his slow smile, was aware of the soldiers silently closing in upon them all. She flung them a glance, startled, looked again at the officer.

"Leon! What do you mean?" She stood surcharged with rage, chagrin, dismay, her emotions warring for utterance. "Oh! You—you Judas! You said you would die for me—"

"No, no; for love, my *doña*," said the officer purringly. "For love, yes, but for you—no! When I die, then I die for Mexico. You thought I'd sell my honor by betraying my general? Bah! Cos knows all about your treachery—rather, suspects it. Come, *señor*," and he gave Kenly a sudden sharp look. "Resistance will be of no use. General Cos is expecting us; it is not far. Corporal! Look to this woman."

Kenly, at first stupefied, still had no words, no voice. It was not his affair; he was watching a frightful struggle end here in the obscurity, a struggle of this woman who had no heart, no conscience, against the tentacles which had enveloped her. General Cos was dominant over everything. He himself had run into a blind alley; the dice had again fallen wrong. What, now, of Josefa? Well, she would not suffer.

There was no outcry; under the lantern, Doña Maria showed white as death, silent. She was desperate, gathering force, seeking with agile brain some outlet.

"Watch her, corporal."

The corporal saluted, at her elbow, his men ready. Contemptuously, Doña Maria gathered cloak about hips; the sunlight was gone out of her face; she was old, unlovely, blotched with suppressed fury. Yet she still tried to extricate herself.

"I, to a corporal? You compliment me. Leon! Listen to me. It was a trap for this fool of an Americano. Once you departed with him, I meant to fly to the general, tell him all, have this fool shot quickly as he deserved, the Texans trapped as they waited by the creek—I demand that you take me to the general! Let him hear my story!"

The sleek officer shrugged, amusedly.

"Blow north, blow south; what matter? Talk to him? Never fear; he's ready for you, my girl. Thought you'd ruin me like many another, eh? God knows where your lies end and truth begins; I care not. *Soldados!* Surround them. Look out for her knife; if she pulls it, tie her up. Forward!"

The route lay to the Veramendi house.

I T W A S still early. Later, music and dancing, a ball, gay uniforms and lovely or unlovely women—but now, business. General Cos was in his headquarters.

The officer, Leon, marched in his exhibit and saluted with a brisk word. "I have done as the general directed. She was sending him to the Tejanos to tell them of your going to the Alamo at midnight—to have them await you at the river." Curt and brief, expressing everything; treachery of the woman, willingness of the prisoner, trust of the general in himself. A man of parts, this Leon.

But not for him were Kenly's eyes. Not for the gold-laced general, smiling with slow craft and triumph; but for the other man sitting there at the table—the olive cheeks, the thin nose and full lips, the upturned mustache, the air of cool dignity, the eyes staring at them in appraisal, in recognition. From Doña Maria burst a word.

"Rodrigo! Don Rodrigo!"

General Cos stirred, took over the situation. He motioned Leon, told him to wait. He leaned back, surveyed Kenly with a quizzical smile and a nod, and had the air of complacent satisfaction. Doña Maria stamped her foot.

"Well? I can explain all this, my general. This silly Leon—"

"Is a shrewd fellow, my dear," cut in Cos, smiling.

"I am tired." She affected a bold play now. "Am I a prisoner or a lady, to be treated as such? When I had arranged to put the Texan leaders into your hands—"

"Your pardon; you may, of course, sit down. In any case, you're destined to have a long rest," and Cos broke into slow laughter. "As for you, *Señor Americano*—"

"That girl was in his cell, Excellency," said the officer, Leon, as the general paused. "The one—ah, you comprehend, my general."

"So? There are too many women in our affairs," observed Cos musingly. "They meddle; they should leave it to the priest to say mass. Come, my honest Americano, my lieutenant—for you are lieutenant still. You have a certain courage; damme, but you're a *caballero!* You see," and his voice fell upon the room amused, unhurried, "I know everything. Two errands you were offered this same night, eh? You, in the uniform of Mexico, to capture me; you, in that same uniform, to post the rebels to catch me—tut, tut! And yet, I clapped you into a cell, that is quite true."

"Will you listen to me?" intervened Doña Maria. Cos gave her one look.

"Shut up. Speak once more before you are addressed, and you'll be taken out by this officer and confined." His gaze came back to Kenly. "You're not hanging to a tree, or facing a squad of rifles—why? Because you spoke as you did, the last time you stood here. For one reason at least. For another, you have a friend. But you're a dangerous guest. I shall dispose of you."

"The choice seems to be yours," Kenly replied coolly. "But

you'll kindly understand that I'm no spy, and that I did not desert under fire."

"I understand more than you think," retorted the general. "All you Americanos and Tejanos seem to think that we of Spanish blood are fools. Well! Your cellmate, who broke prison this evening, is captured; he goes to hard labor until it pleases me to shoot him. You know Captain Estramadura, I believe?"

Kenly's gaze flickered to Don Rodrigo, whose steady countenance expressed nothing.

"I have that honor," said Kenly, half ironically.

"So. Our good captain is going to Mexico to find *El Presidente*; he will be glad of your company. I shall be glad to do without it. Your business goes to His Excellency, and you with it, and the whole cursed affair. Ha! What is that?"

The air of the room shuddered. There was a sudden roar, then another; cannon. A crackling of rifles, shrill yells. The clamor swelled as an aide plunged into the room with hasty salute.

"My general! The Tejanos have not marched away. They are attacking the street barricades—"

General Cos came to his feet.

"Captain Estramadura, get out of here at once, you and Lieutenant Leon take this Americano with you. If he resists, shoot him. Lieutenant Leon! See that the horses are supplied, and all else. When they have departed, report to me."

He hurried from the room, calling sharp orders to his aides. Kenly turned, met the gaze of Don Rodrigo, who had risen and was tapping a pistol-butt. Doña Maria had spoken wildly, but Don Rodrigo paid her no attention.

"Well?" His gaze was fastened on Kenly. "Do we go as friends or as enemies?"

"Have it your own way," rejoined Kenly. Don Rodrigo suddenly smiled, and extended his hand.

"Come, then, *caballero*—come! Devil take me, but we've riding ahead of us and the tattoo of hell at our heels!"

And the Texan rifles, the cannon at the barricades, made

answer. Ben Milam was there in the night, with death and victory and eternal glory awaiting him.

But for Kenly—something else, as the dice of destiny fell and clattered.

CHAPTER XIII

THE OUTER premises of the Veramendi house were in tremendous confusion, with messengers hurrying, officers darting about, the shout of orders and a babel of voices from the nearby streets.

The eastern sky in the direction of the Alamo was fitfully illumined by the red thunders of cannon. At right angles, or to the northward, and so close as to be in the very town, sounded the cheers and cracking rifles of the attack; to these the muskets of the defense made reply. Kenly knew that much time must have passed, there in the stately mansion—much time, few words. Midnight had crept on toward morning, though as yet the dawn was far distant.

As he was hastily trotted along, there came a whistle and shrill of grape and balls in the air overhead. The streets were filled with figures, with voices.

"But they are devils, these Tejanos!"

"They are attacking the Garza house now. They will be here next, if they are not stopped!"

"Did you see that poor soldier with his eyes shot out—"

"Ha!" said Don Rodrigo calmly to the lieutenant. "A wild night, it appears."

"And a wilder day ahead," replied Leon with a short laugh. "Until we can put the guns and the cavalry to work with morning, at least. Then you'll see these ruffians swept away. Damn these cholo soldiers of ours!"

The word stabbed at Kenly. The cholo soldiery, halfbreed and criminal conscripts, were bad enough inside. Outside, the Texans, who must be fighting from house to house, from barricade to barricade; and Josefa in the midst, there in Zambrano Row. It was like a twist of steel in his brain.

Abruptly, without a word, he swerved in his step, burst through the men around him, flung himself in the other direction. Instantly forms closed in. Kenly fought them aside, savage fist and boot making play—until a pistol-butt thudded against his skull, dazing him. They had him then, held him quivering, cursing.

"Come, *señor!*" Don Rodrigo spoke at his ear, sternly. "Have some sense. If one side doesn't shoot you, the other will. What is it? A woman, perhaps?"

"It is she—in there," panted Kenly, his brain reverting to normal.

"Well, she is safe, I promise you. Now, there is haste; must I tie you or not?"

"No."

With this half-promise, Don Rodrigo was satisfied. Again Kenly was thrust along hurriedly, prisoner none the less. The detour from the Veramendi house ended at a group of soldiers in waiting; dragoons, these.

Kenly climbed into a saddle as ordered. His feet, once in the stirrups, were linked by a rawhide thong passed under the belly of the horse. He made no protest: A thick cloak was tossed him and he fastened it about his neck. Something very like a stupor of despair was upon him.

An "*Adios*" for the lieutenant, hasty mounting, and with the reins of his horse taken by a soldier, Kenly felt the animal heave up and away with the others.

They went at speed, rattling through a crooked street, swerving into the main plaza, skirting dark San Fernando church and crossing, breakneck, the Military Plaza. Here firefly lights swarmed in scurrying alarm amid the murk, and confusion echoed back trebly from stone walls. Out of the Plaza now, and thundering over a bridge of San Pedro creek. Then, with abrupt turn and unslackened rein, the party gained the open country beyond and the road winding in the darkness.

The clamor of combat behind had lessened. To Kenly's sense of locality, they were striking to the southward, the hooves thudding sharply on the road. Presently Don Rodrigo dropped back to ride at Kenly's knee.

"You are yourself again? Forgive me that tap with the pistol."

Kenly's futile anger mounted, and ebbed again.

"Where are we going, then?"

"My despatches are for Santa Anna, at Monclova."

"Where is that?"

"A hundred and fifty leagues, and more. First to Laredo at the Rio Grande, then on into the south."

"And I?" queried Kenly bitterly.

"You, like the despatches, are for His Excellency."

"At Monclova?"

"*Quien sabe?*" evaded the other with careless tone. "I am on duty there, at least; we shall wait and see." And with this, Don Rodrigo spurred ahead once more.

Four hundred miles, then; and at the end of such journey— what? "Your business goes to His Excellency," had said Cos, which might mean much or little. In the meantime there was fighting in Bejar, and a Jim Bowie yet to be satisfied with explanations. Kenly rippled with low-voiced curses. Every way a crooked way, no path before him straight and true, everywhere frustration!

The party swept on at steady gallop, splashing through streams, keeping good pace as though anxious to leave behind any chance of marauding Texans. Kenly nodded in the saddle, thankful that he had the cloak; the December air was raw and chili.

Between naps his thoughts dwelt curiously on Don Rodrigo.

"Silence him, Leon!"

The captain seemed friendly enough, but this spelled little of definite consolation. How would this friendliness be directed in shaping his future? Kenly had rather take his chances in Bejar than in Mexico with Santa Anna.

SKY AND earth at last brightened with the dawn. The morning breeze flitted cold out of a wide desert overhung by a pale sky. Halt was made to loosen girdles, breathe and rest the horses, and munch upon ration breakfast. Of San Antonio, the north was empty; not even a film of smoke rose there.

Don Rodrigo joined Kenly, sitting beside him, sharing food and water.

"I regret the things that have happened to you," he proffered after a bit. "Still, that rascally American and Doña Maria are accounted for; I think you've come off better than they. She was behind much of what took place. A devious woman, that, spurred by hatred and jealousy into hot folly, and trying vainly to act as the power behind the throne. Bah! She wasn't made for the part. The despatches I bear for *El Presidente* will speak of you, among other things."

"No doubt," Kenly sarcastically replied. He could not understand this man, these people of alien race and blood. He could not fathom their ways, their easy, unhurried actions. Americans would have had that silver mine found and gripped long ere this, yet they dallied, hung fire, procrastinated. True, the revolution was largely responsible for this. None the less, the difference remained.

"Cos said that I had a friend," Kenly observed. "Who is it?"

Don Rodrigo laughed in his silky fashion.

"It may be himself, for one. You're the kind of man to please him; he has the heart of a soldier, at least. Or—it may be this Captain Estramadura to whom you speak. Why not? Again, it may even be *El Presidente*. He knows by this time that you risked all to rescue that girl from the Indian—she was not sent with his knowledge, you see. He is interested in her, very definitely."

"He can spare his interest," snapped Kenly.

"So?" The other studied him reflectively for a moment. "I advise you to let him manage that affair; you have enough to settle. I begin to understand, and I offer you the warning of a friend. Lieutenant Leon mentioned the girl having been in the *carcel* with you. And your break for freedom—so that was it?"

"Yes," Kenly replied bluntly.

"Well, nothing of all this to Santa Anna—upon your life!" cautioned Don Rodrigo gravely. "Stifle heart and feelings; seek fortune and honor alone. That's the motto these days. And truly, this trip may mean much to you. How'd you like to ride with me to find the San Saba silver? I've requested the favor."

"The silver be damned," said Kenly.

"Oh, assuredly; just the same, it awaits us. I'm quite honest about it, *amigo*, but I'm only a captain. General Cos has plans; so has the president. As for Bowie, he's a rebel with a price on his head, and the silver's lost to him. The mines are for Mexico."

"Or for Texas," said Kenly significantly.

Don Rodrigo, smiling, caressed his mustache.

"Texas? That is a name, no more. This insurrection, by rough men who wish to make their own state laws, will soon be put down; even if not, Texas would still be part of Mexico. However, these rebels will soon be destroyed." Don Rodrigo came to his feet. "We must go. I am responsible for you, *señor*. A little farther on, I shall let you ride freely, as a friend; for the moment, I take no chances."

"That suits me," said Kenly. The other shrugged.

"You'll not want to run for it when you see this desolate country. And whither would you run—to Bejar? By this time the rebels there have been cut to pieces. They'll be destroyed without mercy. Then, with all northern Mexico pacified, you and I will enjoy our little treasure hunt. Well, see you later," and the captain gayly strode away.

The party resumed the southward road, Kenly, a little enlightened by this conversation, began to glimpse fresh hope. The magic of a few words opened to him a new vista, unguessed possibilities. That Don Rodrigo was really friendly, had really put in a good word for him, that General Cos himself was not hostile, could be credited, The silver? Why not, if Bowie lost claim to it? He had tried to make his peace with Jim Bowie and had failed; indeed, Bowie must now be more bitter than ever against him. But this could not be helped.

PERHAPS DON RODRIGO'S proposition was the best way out after all. With Texas and the Mexican government reconciled by force of arms, with Bowie out of it, with Santa Anna gone into the south again, with himself employed—

What of Josefa, then? What of prosperity, happiness? What were these dark hints of Santa Anna's interest in that girl? Oh, intolerable! Kenly thrust it all aside from his brain. Here was the journey ahead; take it, and forget all else.

The captain's warning had been well based, as he could perceive. A desolate land, this; a bleak, bare, sterile, windy country.

Desert stretches extending from lonely river to lonely river, as futile, empty, hopeless, as his own heart.

The days fell behind with unending miles and blank horizons.

Kenly was no longer tethered, was no longer a prisoner; his relations were on a most friendly footing with Don Rodrigo. He grew to admire and respect the man.

The pace had been reduced to conserve the flagging beasts. The *jornadas*, or daily journeys, were regulated by the forage and the water. The men talked and jested, with frequent speculation as to what had taken place back there at Bejar, The Tejanos who had not been shot or captured—which was the same thing—would still be running. And when General Don Antonio Lopez de Santa Anna came in person, with the picked troops of Mexico—eh, Pedro? *Caramba!*

He might make himself president of North America!

Sense of time or place was lost in loneliness and vast horizons, until at last grew the town called Laredo. Here, beside the Rio Grande; a forsaken, ugly adobe village which seemed to be a gathering place for brawlers, smugglers, bravos and army deserters. Wretched quarters, while the dragoons swaggered and made merry. Stop was made for two days, to recruit saddle animals and rest weary muscles, and then on again for Monclova. Fifty leagues more, now of worse desert than ever, rugged and hard on man and beasts.

Late in the afternoon of the second day from Laredo, a dot came rapidly enlarging on the back trail. A rider with a led horse; a single rider spurring, belly to earth, coming on as if the devil pursued.

"A courier who spares no horse-flesh!" ejaculated Don Rodrigo. "*Diantre!* Here comes news, then." He swung his mount across the trail. "Halt, you! What haste?"

The rider was a sergeant, red of lids and grimy of skin. He threw his horse to its haunches, the second animal swerving and recoiling.

"To *El Presidente*," gasped the sergeant. "*Violento extraordi-*

nario—special courier at all speed. I will change. Bear a hand with the saddle, one of you."

He tumbled off, while two of the dragoons came to change the saddle from one sweated animal to the other.

"What news? Out with it!" snapped Don Rodrigo.

"Bad, *señor capitan*. The accursed Tejanos have taken Bejar,"

"What?" The word burst from Don Rodrigo, was echoed by the dragoons.

"True enough," asserted the courier. "They fought like devils. They burrowed like rats. From house to house, from room to room, right through Zambrano Row."

The word hit Kenly. He listened, intent, while the sergeant swigged a little water and then went on.

"They drove us all. Artillery? They had none; their rifles were deadly. They moved untouched amid cannon fire, and we died. Cos surrendered from the Alamo, on terms. Clear the road! I go. *Adios!*"

He was into the saddle again, with a groan and a curse. His mount leaped to the spur; the second horse lunged to the jerk of the neck-rope.

"Go then with God," called Don Rodrigo, "or with the devil."

He swung his horse, ordered his men into file, rode at Kenly's stirrup.

"Bejar taken! It is incredible. It is past belief," he murmured, stunned by the news. "When *El Presidente* hears of this, I should hate to be General Cos."

For the remainder of the road to Monclova he was moody, his Spanish pride piqued, his soldier's pride mortified. In Kenly's brain there re-echoed the words: "Zambrano Row." An ill place that, for Josefa, with the Texans and the soldiers at grips! But Don Rodrigo had declared she was in safety. She had been released from that cell. In case of the worst, she would have seen Jim Bowie.

SO, FINALLY, the wastes of sand and rocks and scattered

chaparral gave space for Monclova. Its flat-roofed stone and adobe buildings clustered on the horizon, then drew apart, as though to welcome them.

"Here we rest," announced Don Rodrigo to Kenly. "My despatches will be forwarded, if Santa Anna is not here. You and I await him. Thank heaven it's not that vile Laredo! This is a place of some comfort."

The old presidio of Monclova was heavily garrisoned anew, grimy with the dust-clouds of provision trains and baggage wagons and marching men. Troops were in waiting. All was bustle and excitement, and ever the word was Santa Anna. *El Presidente* was coming from the south with his army. A great army, mustered from afar, for Bejar; to take Bejar as one would pinch a candle, to send the Texan rebels scuttling for their holes. What would they, a scant few hundred, do against this great army of Mexico led by Santa Anna himself? One would see, there in the north!

This talk, boast and threat and jubilation, in street and dram shop and garrison, dinned upon Kenly's ears. A Legion of Honor had been created—silver crosses for the lucky privates who won it in Texas, gold crosses for officers.

The choicest regiments of dragoons were on the march. His Excellency had a great golden coach—and so it ran, rumor and story running rife.

And His Excellency came. Aides galloped into town with the news. Streets began to boil, rooftops began to crowd with faces. Flags blew out, colors of white, red and green hung fair. The long dust-haze drew in from the south, the dust hanging over the glinting bayonets and lance-tips. Five thousand, six thousand, ten thousand men—who could say? Then the golden coach indeed, girded by a dazzling cavalcade of officers, prancing through the crazed streets for the presidio quarters.

"*Viva Mexico! Viva Santa Anna! Viva El Presidente!*"

It was next morning when Don Rodrigo, accoutered at his best, strode into the room Kenly occupied, with click of busy heels and brisk announcement.

"His Excellency will receive us at once, *amigo*. The aide says he's in great good humor; it augurs well. Come along!"

So Destiny rang the bell. Kenly shrugged, spruced up the shabby rags of his uniform, and accompanied the other.

Santa Anna, naturally, occupied the best house in town. Ceremony was required here; the personal staff alone formed a small army. But Santa Anna saw fit to receive them alone, in his headquarters office. The escorting aide withdrew, the door closed.

El Presidente was seated at a table strewn with papers; a sheaf of documents was before him, under his eyes and fingers. His rather slight figure was held upright by the close uniform that stiffly trussed him to the ears.

A very war lord, he, all ablaze with gold lace, epaulets, decorations.

His manner was gracious, extremely so; yet Kenly instantly sensed a thrill of danger in the air. In the deliberate smile which almost disarmed him, in the bright flickering eyes, in the studied poise, lay peril intangible.

Santa Anna could be most charming. Now his smile, his address to Kenly, matched with words that were almost jocular.

After the first salutations he ignored Don Rodrigo and bent his entire smiling attention upon the American.

"Ah, the valiant recruit officer with the flat nose. Come, I hear serious things about you, charges of desertion, of spying! What have you to say to them?"

There was only one response to make.

"That they are false, Excellency."

"Indeed? And yet the papers speak for themselves." Santa Anna mused, then looked up with quicker utterance. "You conspired against the person of General Cos?"

"Well, why not?" rejoined Kenly bluntly. "He used his power against my person."

The quick black eyes narrowed.

"I see you are bold. Very well; it is a great pity your conspiracy did not succeed; we could have spared that gentleman. A great pity!" Santa Anna swallowed an onrush of bubbling emotion. Kenly suddenly realized that he was facing a volcano, a veritable volcano, merely surface-cooked. This smile, this calm, were all assumed. "Well, no matter about that. There is something else. You have, it appears, been made use of by others, and not by my desires—no matter about that, either. You are one of those men who possess a blundering destiny. Is that not so?"

Kenly smiled. "Destiny can be averted or conquered, Your Excellency, as you have yourself made manifest."

MOMENTARY GRATIFICATION at the compliment; it fled quickly. Again, more harshly, Kenly could sense danger lurking beneath the surface words.

"Let us see. General Cos is good enough to suggest that as soon as these Texan adventurers are crushed, you and Captain Estramadura here should be sent to locate and reopen those silver mines of which you know. The previous expedition did not, it seems, meet with a satisfactory conclusion. Don Rodrigo, I understand, proposes your company for him. You are two men of a kind, and dependable. In the meantime you are yourself to be detained somewhere in the interior. How does this appeal to you?"

Kenly groped his way blindly, the peril closer, at his very elbow.

"That might be feasible," he ventured.

"So?" Santa Anna had been toying with another paper. "I have a letter here from another source, one Doña Maria—whom I think you know. Besides certain appeals to me, she also favors me with a bit of gossip."

Suddenly, without warning, it was the eruption. Santa Anna rose, hands clenching the table edge, eyes swiftly ablaze; his chair went scraping. The steady, inscrutable smile had left his lips. They were parted now for the flash of white wolf-teeth and a flood of caustic words, snarling and deadly.

"So! In the very room with you, what? Companion for the night; and you would play the lover after I had myself arranged for the girl! In the very room, the very cell with you, in man's attire—"

"Who says a word against her, lies," blared out Kenly, white to the lips. The other glared at him.

"Silence, or you'll be gagged," snapped Santa Anna, and meant it. "I am no weakling, Cos. You take too much to yourself for having rescued the girl. This business has gone far enough; as for Doña Maria, I can well believe that her insinuations are lies. I remember that girl's face. I remember her. I have planned to marry her upon reaching Bejar. And you—you—"

Marry her! The words brought silence upon the room. Santa Anna was over his quick outburst. He sank back into his chair, contemplating Kenly with thoughtful eyes. In the pause, Kenly caught the rapid breathing of Don Rodrigo, beside him. Then those dark, evil eyes kindled with crafty amusement.

"You, my fine Americano, shall be present at the wedding; you shall then be shot. You will die happy, knowing that the little *señorita* is provided for."

Kenly, tense, fists clenched, features drawn, suddenly caught sight of a flutter in the curtains behind Santa Anna's chair. Something moved there. A glint of gold lace, the glitter of eyes; an officer stationed there with a pistol, his brain realized. He kept a grip on himself.

"As for Cos and his recommendations—ah!" Santa Anna went livid at the name. He snarled again, erupted in a burst of objurgation. "That coward, that sheep! To surrender fifteen hundred men to a handful of ragged farmers! Trade his honor for a parole not to fight again! Do I take advice from such a source?"

His gaze lit upon Kenly again. With a fierce impatience, he dismissed all pretense.

"I thought he understood; you were not to return from that

silver hunt. Bah! And now he admires your impudence, he sends
you to me. He admires you! Well, I do not. You, Captain Estramadura, are now responsible for this fellow. Take him away;
bring him to me at Bejar, or before then if I order it. I hold you
accountable for him—your life shall answer for it if he escapes.
You comprehend? That is your sole duty."

Don Rodrigo saluted, a little white. He knew when Santa
Anna meant business. The two were abruptly dismissed. Don
Rodrigo led Kenly to his own quarters in black silence. Not
until the door was closed upon them did he speak.

"In these rages, he is like a madman," said Don Rodrigo,
simply. He took a chair, motioned Kenly to another, regarded
him fixedly. "That damned Doña Maria has her finger in it
again, eh? And *El Presidente* jokes; these jokes of his are not
nice. A wedding guest and then the firing squad; he means it.
But wait till he fronts Cos—then you'll hear cursing! He's been
absolutely crazy about this girl, I hear; he's given orders regarding her. That rascally aide of his, Muñoz, has told me."

"But the man's married!" said Kenly blankly. Don Rodrigo
laughed.

"Bah! He's dictator of Mexico, and his wife has grown tire-
some to him—he takes up with any woman who eyes him. This
time it's serious. Muñoz tells me that orders have been sent
Cos to bring the girl to meet the army at Laredo. The wedding
will be at Bejar, eh?"

KENLY SCARCELY heard. That wedding—a very gift
laid beside a barren trail! So Santa Anna would joke with death
and dishonor? Good! Bejar it should be, and a joke with a
conclusion not anticipated by *El Presidente*. An idea to feed
upon. Meantime, let Mexico furnish subsistence and transport.
Kenly was not minded to court further disaster by taking, alone
and unaided, that back trail through hostile desert.

"Eh?" Don Rodrigo caught the blaze in his eyes, the stiffen-
ing of muscles under impact of tense thought. He spoke gravely.
"Listen, *amigo*; you think of escape? But consider me. I have

come to know you well. You are a true *caballero*. If you escape, then I die; that is certain. Give me your parole, your word of honor, otherwise you go forward to Bejar in irons."

"Very well," said Kenly. "You have my word, as long as I'm left at liberty. Always subject to withdrawal."

"It is understood," returned Don Rodrigo, and twisted his mustache. "And now for a drink, eh? Then on to Bejar!"

On to Bejar! The words ran like fire. The bugles voiced them. The camps were struck. The army was off in columns—foot, horse, artillery and baggage. And Kenly under loose guard in the command of Captain Estramadura.

The troops, after their march from the south, were the worse for wear. Thin cotton uniforms for men traversing the high wintry deserts of the north. But Santa Anna was a driver, and from his golden coach drove hard.

The trail, leveled as best might be by a pioneer corps ahead, was scourged by northers and harshened by bitter nights. The trail, littered by exhausted men and beasts, dotted by broken-down wagons, leading on ever to the northward. And the trail's ending at last, with the green line of the Rio Grande between its brown hills, brought finis to the ghastly march of these thousands. And fresh cheers for *El Presidente*, in his coach of luxury, with his bodyguard, his silver service, his special cook, his hampers of wines and choice foods.

Laredo, gateway to Texas, where General Cos and his paroled troops awaited the caustic tongue of the dictator, and waited not in vain.

Kenly, worn out by that last forced march, staggered into the quarters Don Rodrigo found for him and dropped. Hours later he wakened from troubled dreams, to smell food beneath his nose, to see the grinning pock-marked features of Pablo beside him.

"*Señor!* Thanks to the saints that you waken. Here is food—"

"You!" Kenly gripped the brown, broad hand. "Josefa? Where is she?"

"Here, with my mother." Pablo's face sobered.

"I must see her, quickly—"

The broad palm rested on his chest. The steady eyes gave warning.

"Careful, *señor!* I may see her, perhaps; not you or another. Those are the orders. She is to marry *El Presidente.*"

Kenly's laugh was sharp. "Not she! Not Josefa!"

"Well, my mother gives orders; and Colonel Muñoz gives guards, and God knows what will come of it. Josefa is helpless. May the saints forgive me for calling my mother a fool, but that's what she is. Here is food—"

"Thanks, Pablo. You must see Josefa. Tell her I'm all right. Tell her to wait. What happened in Bejar?"

"Fighting day and night. Josefa reached the Alamo safely with us. The general took her and my mother when we marched out under terms. I will tell Josefa what you say; but he is *El Presidente*, and there is to be a wedding at Bejar. She is a good girl; she threatens the knife, but this news will slow her hand. I know how things lie between you, but what can I do?"

"Give the message." Kenly forced himself to eat. Josefa here, almost within touch! The thought burned at him; but he was older now, harder, more patient. He saw where folly might ruin all things. "What became of that Americano, Devore?"

"Oh, that Mateo?" Pablo grinned again. "He's been put to hard labor, working on the road—no, he was not shot. He came with us from Bejar. Well, *señor*, I must go. The march begins at once, they say—"

True enough; the thousands were pouring forth, short of food, cursing the icy wind, yet driven by the master.

Kenly saw no more of Pablo, with reason. He had a brief glimpse of Josefa, in a coach with her mother, a white wan face alight with her quick spirit. Don Rodrigo got him clothes—no uniform, but stout harsh garments to replace his rags.

O N T O Bejar, with Cos himself turned about, regardless of parole; Santa Anna, in raging fury, forced him to break it, and his troops with him. Blistering sun and sand and rocks by day, icy winds and stinging cold by night. Santa Anna in one rage after another, his aides flying about with hard orders, driving, ever driving. The pioneers were out constantly. All prisoners were set to work upon the cut-bank fords and on the roads.

Kenly among them, for Santa Anna saw him riding along with Don Rodrigo and loosed vials of wrath upon his head. Torn from his horse, stripped of his serape, he was put under guard and set to work, He could exchange no words with Don Rodrigo, but their eyes met for one moment, and in that one look exchanged lay what must be unsaid. Kenly knew he was absolved of his parole.

The columns rolled on, breasting the winds, starving, scrambling, singing, cursing, ever advancing. These were soldiers either to be well driven or well led. Bejar drew nearer, and there were rumors. It was astonishing how rumors came out of the desert and the prairie, sifting through the camps. Spies at work, it might be; the dragoons rode hard and far. The Texans holding Bejar were few in number. They were awaiting reinforcements. There was talk of secession from Mexico, They did not know that this armed host of hardy *valientes*, with *El Presidente* himself, was already close upon them.

The Medina River was less than twenty miles from Bejar.

El Presidente was in a rage again. Dragoons and footmen had crossed; but the cursed Medina, heavy with mud, had swollen bank full and the ammunition wagons were still on the other side. The devil had leagued with these contemptible rebels. *El Presidente* left his coach shelter for his black charger, bloody from the rowels, and rode the river bank, damning the flood, the draggled officers and men. Nothing more could be done until the river flood went down, which would be hours away.

The guards were slack that night, drowsy.

None saw the figure shifting among outstretched forms swathed in serapes from knees to crown. None saw it edging from the fires, slipping through the lines. One sentry alone, full awake, full in the path, gave husky startled challenge.

Then came noises that the rain drowned out, and a dead man turned white face to the wet and blanketed sky. And presently, from the horse-lines, the faint thud-thud of hooves lessening and departed.

CHAPTER XIV

THE RED FLAG

A CARELESS GARRISON, indeed. No outposts in the approaches, no sentries, no patrols on duty.

Thus in the early morning Kenly entered town unchallenged. The mercantile side of the military plaza was spottily lighted; here, as betokened by high-pitched shouts and cries and snatches of song, *tienda* and *cantina, pulqueria* and monte bank were running full chisel.

The fandango continued. He could hear discordant revelry coming from El Plaza de la Constitucion, there beyond the darkly brooding mass of San Fernando church. Twang of smitten string, clash of castanets, stamp of feet, shout and laughter and applause.

Here between the two plazas, Kenly dismounted and briefly hesitated, when a figure wambling down the street addressed him; a sturdy, red-faced man.

"*Como 'sta, hombre!* Say, *mucha señorita*, savvy? Unnerstand? No fandango for me; *mucha señorita*. You know? Will you be takin' me to a fine lass, now?"

"Speak English, do you?" said Kenly. "Never mind the girls. Where can I find Jim Bowie? Who's in command here?"

"Hooray for Texas!" came the maudlin response. "It's like a hard winter ye look, me lad. Who's in command? Devil a soul of us knows. Bowie is by his own account, Travis is by his, and the two of 'em cat and dog. Ward's the name, me lad, Cap'n Ward of Texas, and not so long from Ireland either—"

*Bullets whistled
and screamed.*

"For the love of heaven, where can I find Bowie?" burst forth Kenly.

"And where should he be but takin' his dram like a gentleman along with the rest? Ye'll find him in La Tienda Americana over in the next plaza. Tell him Cap'n Ward gave ye the countersign, which is 'To hell with Santy Anny.'"

Kenly hurried on. He was drenched, thinned by fatigue and privation, hard as iron, burned browner than any Mexican by sun and wind, his hair uncut, his features bearded; a scarecrow object, but so driven by determination that men made way and gave him wondering glances.

American Store it was, but a liquor shop. And deep within it, four men seated as by easy authority. One man Kenly knew, even by profile. Bowie, comfortably slouched, in Mexican velvet jacket, girded with a brace of pistols. Another he knew, the bearded Travis, in trim gray uniform. The third, with back turned? Coonskin cap with stripe-ringed tail, leather hunting shirt, and suspended powder horn—Kenly's mind leaped at a stride five hundred miles to New Orleans and a table there.

Davy Crockett of Tennessee! The fourth man at the table was a stranger.

The room, aflicker with the smoky light of candles, held only these four men and the liquor vendor. From the plaza, the lusty, revelrous, blood-heating music of the fandango swept into the place. Kenly came up to the four, who stared at him with varying gaze. A glance showed that Bowie was ugly drunk, Crockett happily touched, Travis slightly elevated, and the fourth man unaffected, keen-eyed, silent.

"Who's in command here?" demanded Kenly abruptly. His voice seemed to waken recognition. Travis spoke up eying him keenly.

"I command the regulars and artillery; Colonel Bowie the volunteers. What's that to you, sir? Who the devil may you be?"

"Santa Anna's at the Medina with his whole army. It's in flood, but as soon as he can get the ammunition wagons and artillery across, he'll be here."

There was a short burst of laughter. "Likely story," said Travis. "Where'd you pick it up?"

"I was there," said Kenly. "A prisoner. I marched up from Monclova. I tell you, the whole Mexican army is—"

"Ha! You damned renegade—now I know you!" burst out Jim Bowie. His icy blue eyes were two frozen pools, malignant. "This is my man of the knife."

"Hurray!" erupted Crockett with genial good nature. "Have a horn o' liquor, stranger. Thar's something in that thar phiz of yourn—by the Etarnal! You're the feller, sure enough, nose or no nose! Here, warm your gizzard with a horn—"

"Listen to me, you drunken fools!" Kenly's voice drove down at them. The force of his personality, the agony of his brain, the intent, resolute dominance of him, suddenly swept everything aside, held them spellbound.

"I tell you, Santa Anna's got his whole army at your very gates. You call yourselves soldiers! Not a patrol posted, not a sentry. Spies have told him everything. He hoped to cross the river and catch you here at the celebration, tonight. He's with the first column himself—the army's sweeping up in four divisions."

"He's a damned liar," growled Bowie, yet impressed none the less. "How many in his army?"

"Six, seven thousand—I don't know exactly."

"Give the feller a dram and he'll make it ten thousand," said Crockett jovially. "Like a congressman figgerin' votes."

"On the contrary, sir," said Travis with chill mien, "we know Santa Anna cannot get here before the middle of March. There's not an armed Mexican on Texan soil. This cock-and-bull story of yours—"

"One moment, Travis." The fourth man intervened. A countenance open and well favored, a keen, appraising eye. "I'm enough of a lawyer to know when a man speaks the truth. My friend, I'm James B. Bonham of South Carolina. Now, give us your name and let's have this story. Damme if I don't believe there's something in it."

CROCKETT SHOVED out a stool. "Sit down. You're shaking on your pins like a blown gobbler. Here, take this horn—sit down! Talk!"

"I'll not sit in company with the rascal," grunted Bowie, but he sat all the same. Kenly sank on the stool, caught the liquor from Crockett's hand, and downed it.

"My name's Kenly," he said. "I stole out of camp, got a horse, killed a sentry—and got here. Santa Anna aimed to shoot me when we reached Bejar. Cos sent me down as a prisoner, the same night the fighting started here. Gentlemen, you've got to believe me! I tell you the first column's across the Medina!"

"Twenty miles away? Impossible," said Travis, but frowned. Crockett laughed out.

"Cock-a-doodle-do! The boys are cutting pigeon-wings with the gals—most of 'em has sold their rifles for liquor. If Santy Anny's coming, let him come along—"

"This rascal's a damned spy," shot forth Bowie furiously. "Throw him into the guardhouse and investigate him tomorrow!"

"Hold, gentlemen; this warrants attention," intervened Bonham. "If this news is true, Travis, what then?"

"Damned if I know," said Travis bitterly. "We can hold the Alamo until Houston brings up an army. We've men enough."

"Santa Anna knows," said Kenly, "that you've not two hundred and fifty men here."

"Well, we took the town with only three hundred!" snapped Bowie. "And all these talking patriots will send us no help unless Sam Houston can whip 'em into action. But Fannin has four hundred men at Goliad. They'll help."

Suddenly Kenly realized that the tension was lifted. He was believed. He leaned forward and began to speak, rapidly. He told of that march northward, of the Mexican army, its composition, its gossip, its orders of no quarter to rebels.

The four men became intent upon his words. Even Bowie, although not losing that malignant scowl, was now regarding Kenly less than his words, the pictures he was painting. Then, in the midst, Kenly faltered. His animation flagged; the liquor had died out. He refused more. Hunger and exhaustion claimed him.

"What's all this to you?" demanded Travis bluntly.

"I'm an American like yourself," said Kenly. "Through no fault of my own, I've been on the wrong side. Mr. Bowie, here, may not trust me—"

"You bet I don't!" Bowie's fist slammed down on the table. "Into that back room with him, Travis. You hear me? This fellow's up to something. There was some trick to get Cos—I don't remember it now. Black treachery. He failed us there, took to his hole. And now he's back. Hold him in that rear room. What d'ye say, Travis?"

Travis spoke impatiently, with color high. "We're all talking in a circle. At the Medina? I'd have heard of it. More likely, Santa Anna's at the other side the Rio Grande. And yet—"

"Hold him. I demand it!" roared out Bowie, his blue eyes filled with fever glints. "Clap him in that back room and do it now. Let's look into this!"

"I'm not running," and Kenly's gaze swept them disdainfully. Bonham gestured slightly to him, and rose.

"Your pardon, gentlemen. I'd like a word with this man aside."

While Bowie tiraded, Bonham spoke softly, rapidly, at Kenly's ear.

"Sir, your story rings true. Trust me in this. I beg of you; we can do nothing with Colonel Bowie. He's a very ill man. I know the symptoms. He's not responsible for his words. Egad, sir, you look famished! Let me take you into the back room here. I'll have some food sent in, instantly. Meantime we can look into the matter—"

Kenly gave way. Words failed him; he staggered suddenly, and went to pieces. Silently, he turned to the door opening at the back, and Bonham held his arm. A small room like a closet, none too fragrant, a cot along one wall. Then the light was cut off as the door closed. Kenly collapsed on the cot.

A candle-glow in his face, and he saw the lounging Mexican who kept the place putting down a plate of food, with a muttered word. Kenly sat up, wolfed the food ravenously, swigged down the mingled rum and water. The door was closed again. With utter relaxation, careless now of anything that happened, Kenly pressed out the candle wick and let himself fall back on the cot. He was asleep almost at once, to a tumult of argument and dispute from the four voices in the adjacent room.

LATER, HE came wide awake in the darkness. The one window showed pale stars; it was still night, then. Kenly swung feet to floor, stood up, and went to the door. He tried it, found it unlocked, shoved it open.

In the room outside, a candle was guttering on the table. The Mexican was behind his counter, seated, asleep. At the table, head forward on arms, was Bowie, snoring. Sprawled out in a chair, chin sunken on breast, coonskin cap over one eye, was Crockett. A faint gust of tinkling music came from the plaza outside. No sign of Travis or the other man, Bonham. Past the flicker of the sputtering candle showed the faintly gray dawn-darkness.

Kenly stepped forth, drank in the clean, moist air of the street. A great weariness oppressed him, a weariness of body and brain. He turned up the street, at random. His errand here was done. Travis was warned—let him look to it! Sold their rifles for liquor, had they? A fine garrison, this!

An open doorway, a glint of colored lights, drew Kenly's eye. He halted, agape, checked the weary dragging of his feet. Slowly the realization broke upon him. Candles, a red-flickering glint of color; two lights burning there. He was looking in at the open door of the church, straight at the high altar. The snores of men came to him. He stepped inside and saw figures stretched there, no doubt beggars or homeless men. The silence, the distant flickering light, the sudden peace, engulfed him. With a sigh, he sank down and let himself go once more into a drift-ing, dreamless sleep.

A pealing voice, a startled cry, brought him up. Up into daylight, blinking around. A sudden vibrant explosion, a mus-ket-shot; then the clangor of a brazen voice overhead, a bell in the cupola. The sun struck down into the church—the morning was well advanced.

Kenly found himself, not in the church itself as he had thought, but in the entry between the doors. Down the ladder from the tower overhead feet were scrambling, a voice was blurting out something inchoate. Shouts lifted outside, the sluff-sluff of running feet; shrieks of women, cries of children, voices of men.

The roof above him drew Kenly with vague insistence, for no definite reason. He rose, went to the ladder, and mounted. Below came a crunch and crash of doors swung shut. No matter.

The sunlight, warm and glorious and comforting, welcomed him with golden fingers. He came out to the parapet, a lone figure there above the town, his little presence unseen, unguessed by all the world.

To the south, flecks of color caught his eye; out beyond the town, on the heights of the Alazan, fluttering down toward the outskirts, the red and white pennons of lancers. Behind them, a glint and glimmer betokening the dragoons. Two horsemen fleeing in front of these videttes, scouring like mad for Bejar. Santa Anna, then, had come; or at least, his vanguard had come. Unopposed, unthreatened.

Kenly leaned forward a little and looked down upon the town below. In El Plaza de la Constitucion a roil of citizens shouting, running to and fro, gathering in groups and separating again; the slamming of shutters and doors, voices of dismay, confusion, terror.

Beyond, in the Military Plaza, a quick outpouring and gathering, a swelling of rallying ranks. So close that in the clear ardent sunlight Kenly could see the faces and figures clearly, Travis, with his red plume of waving hair, Bowie, the sturdy figure of Crockett; mustering, ordering, forming the ranks. Flash of sword, glint of musket and rifle, and a ringing American cheer, a wild "Hurrah!" They set off on the march. Not out toward the enemy, but off toward the Alamo, a half-mile distant. Passing the church, on through El Plaza de la Constitucion, on for the river and the fortress there. Civilians swung in behind the column, women, slaves or servants.

Kenly glanced south again. The lancers were at the bottom of the slopes now, and behind them a company or two of dragoons, line upon line, with bugle notes adrift in the tremulous, sun-hot air.

Now for the Alamo—ah! Clear and distinct he found it upon its gentle rise beyond the peaceful river. A flag was running up; the flag of that Mexico whose constitution Santa Anna had destroyed, and for which Texas fought, green and red and white, with the date of the Constitucion midway. Figures of men were busy outside the walls, gathering cattle into the wide enclosures, bringing provisions from dwellings; and along the barracks on the right of the chapel, tending the guns and swinging them about. A few figures in one battery—that of the volatile Captain Ward, had Kenly known it—ready and alert. All else wild confusion.

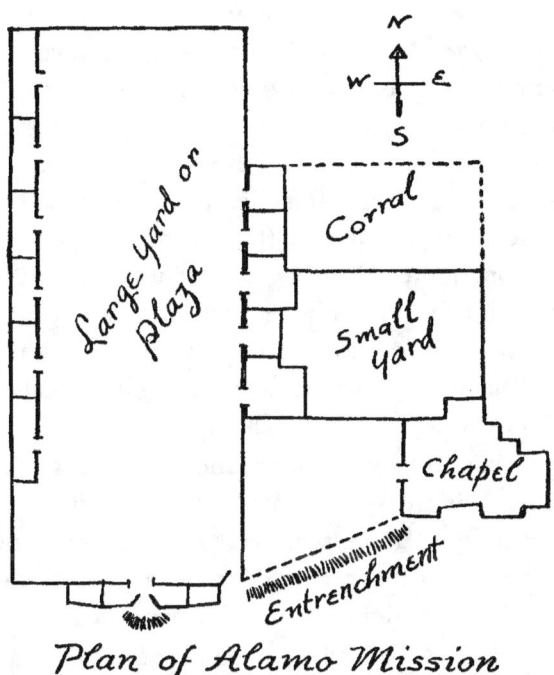

Plan of Alamo Mission

NOW THE column evacuating Bejar appeared crossing the river. Horsemen outflung to sweep in the herded cattle, others bearing straight ahead. Now from the town a single man galloping, spurring from the rear. He carried a baby; behind him a woman, his wife, arms clasped about him. Blue uniform, sword dangling; an officer, this. "Dickinson! Hurray for Dickinson!" lifted distant acclaim.

Kenly started suddenly; then relaxed again, his brown, thinned features hard and set. No impulse now, but reason and reason enough; Josefa! He had sped his bolt for Texas last night and somehow it had failed. No matter. Now for Josefa. What place better than this, unsuspected, unobserved? A little hunger or thirst was of small moment. A little patience were well spent. He settled down, a grimly intent figure.

The lancers deployed, the dragoons broke serried ranks, searching byways and approaches, circling out about the town. Through the streets, the populace swarmed in eagerness. "*Viva! Viva Santa Anna!*" lifted the voices. Thud of hooves, jingle of equipment, blowing breath of bugles. A column came down the street into the plaza; dragoons with green jackets, red *calzoneras* or pantaloons slashed with white, cuirassier helmets, carbines and sabers. File after file, filling the street, forming ranks in the plazas; and behind them came file upon file again, more dragoons, more lancers, swinging lines of ragged infantry. The plazas and the streets boiled with men and officers. The church itself rose like a rock in the surf; the voices, the clink, clatter and clank of spurred heels, tramping hooves and rolling wheels struck Kenly in the face like spray.

He drew back. He was more cautious now; as those troops marched in, their eyes were searching skyline and rooftops. He looked out at the Alamo. Upon the commanding ground to the north of the little fort appeared pennons, a glitter of cannon, a flag and the growing lines of tents. An armed camp here.

Kenly sank down behind the parapet and dozed again reckless what happened, now content to wait. If any mounted to this spot, there were timbers, brick, tools, over in the far corner, where some repair work had been abandoned, he could always hide himself there. The spot was ideal.

In the streets below, the march unending as the sun lifted high in zenith. Wagons, howitzers, the supply train. More troops. All Mexico flooding in vengeance upon the paltry levy of undisciplined rebels who had fled those dancing pennons to refuge behind fortress walls. Scant refuge there from Mexico!

Kenly dozed. Afternoon drew on. Fresh voices rose, and this

time lifted him to the parapet again. "*Viva El Presidente! Viva Santa Anna!*"

A regimental band, or what was left of it, swinging along with brave stir of drums and trumpets. Behind, no longer coached but mounted on black charger, the gold-laced figure of the dictator, gallantly staffed by glittering aides. He came and went and vanished from Kenly's sight, and another guarded convoy drew in. The carriage, here, for which Kenly looked with devouring eyes. An aide was in charge of its escort. He watched it swing off and seek a house behind the palace of the governors, and halt there.

His pulses leaped. Hungrily he saw two figures descend, giantess and slender girl; they vanished within the house. The carriage went on. A sentry was posted in the street. Kenly sank down again. Josefa! At least, he knew where she was. He sat there, glowering, resolute brain quelling swift impulse; awaiting the set of sun, the darkness. Meet the devil halfway, indeed? Meet him before he started! This night he would burst the barriers of his evil destiny, once and for all. God would send the time, as Josefa said—had sent it already.

A bugle aroused him, its quavering notes swimming sweetly on the golden air of afternoon. Kenly rose and looked. Two officers with a bugler orderly bearing a white flag; they had halted, between the river bridge and the Alamo. From the fort came out two figures to meet them. Who? Too far to see, yet Kenly guessed at the erect carriage of Bowie. A moment's talk; then the Mexican officers wheeled about and galloped for the town. The bugler, trailing the white flag, pressed them closely.

A belch of smoke from the southwest corner of the fort walls. The heavy voice of the cannon rolled across the river and through Bejar, and in its wake followed a thin, distant medley of cheers. Then a shell from a Mexican battery on the east edge of town arched athwart the horizon and raised a burst of dust inside the fort. Other guns took the refrain. They raised other bursts of dust and spotted the fort walls with dun puffs of earth and smoke.

KENLY WATCHED, thrilled despite himself, until suddenly he swung around. Feet were mounting the ladder; there were exultant, laughing voices. He had just time to fling himself at the far corner and crouch there.

Two privates and a corporal; here was a color squad, but the colors they convoyed were not those of Mexico. They paused as they fitted their burden to the halyards.

"This for rebels, eh, Diego?"

"They can read it well enough, by the saints! Up with it, *hombres!*"

To the staff above the cupola; of the bell-tower it fluttered. With a laughing salute, a jeer, a gesture toward the Alamo, the squad departed again.

A square flag of solid red. Its crimson field, lifting in the light breeze, was a blotch of blood against the blue sky. It was the flag of "no quarter." Another like unto it fluttered out at the camp on the height north of the Alamo, as the sun descended. A mute but terrible voice that silenced the cannon with its eloquence.

Dusk descended. Upon the plain, the rising ground, twinkled the red Mexican campfires. Kenly paced restlessly, now to survey the Alamo, now to peer over at that street door where a sentry walked. He was chafed raw with the anxiety and bitter determination that filled him; it was hard to wait. The dusk descended into darkness and thin mist lifting from the river and channels. A blare of music and song drifted up from the town, the odors of food cooking were thick upon the air.

It was time—it was time! The tension broke. Kenly hurled himself at the ladder, paused for a moment, got himself in hand, crushed down his blazing eagerness. No slips now! He was done with all that.

He went down, he found himself in the entry. The outer doors were closed and locked. Inside the church, lights glittered as before. A few people, dim shapes in the obscurity, came and went by an open side door. He strode for it, passed the figures without a look, gained the door and was in the street outside, fingers gripping palms, his heart hot.

With all these thousands here, his presence was unnoted, lost. The town was quieting, save for ribald gayety in the shops skirting the plazas. Kenly strode on fast and heedless of anything but the resolve smoldering within him. The street, there; he swung into it. Empty, save for the sentry before the door, musket on shoulder. Empty! None to see, none to interfere. Kenly laughed harshly as the sentry stared at him and came to challenging halt. He made no response, save with a gesture that caused the fellow to frown in scowling bewilderment.

Then the blow, merciless; and another. The slump of body against wall, the clatter of falling musket. A leap to the door, hand and knee to the weight of it. Into the house burst Kenly, and upon candlelight. A black figure there, kneeling, the light of the wick touching a crucifix. The startled face, the gasping cry of recognition, and the candle snuffed under quick hard hand.

For a moment they clung, breathless, incredulous. Then Kenly whispered, "Quick! You go with me?"

"Thank God!" she half sobbed. "I have the knife—"

"Keep it. Come along. To the Alamo. We can make it!"

There was none to see or interfere.

CHAPTER XV

TEXAS IS BORN

"THEY WON'T hold off—much longer," said Bowie. He spoke with difficulty.

He had been lying here for the past week, on his cot in the alcove room. An upper room, this, at the chapel end of the barracks running out from the Alamo. Kenly had just come in. Josefa, devoted nurse, hovered close.

Bowie's twin pistols lay ready to the grasp; curved handles and long straight barrels, like moccasin snakes prepared to rise and strike. From his shirt front shone the silvered haft of the great knife; peace offering, at last accepted. Death lurked unseen in pistols and blade, but it lay plain to sight in the stern and wasted visage, in the cold thinned hand, of the man himself. His lungs, he complained, were bound with an iron band. Pain in breathing, sharp chills, fever, exhaustion. His voice was a rasping, fading whisper.

"What news? They didn't—lay into us quite—so hard today."

"No," said Kenly. "A week's cannonade and not a man of us hit. They've made a breach at the northwest corner of the plaza, though. Travis is filling it."

"Ammunition?"

Kenly shook his head. "Pretty low. We're saving the ball and grape."

"Holding off, are they? I mean—to hold out. They'll have—to come up here—I can't come down." A faint smile touched the dying face.

"Oh, Don Santiago, don't talk, don't talk!" cried Josefa softly. The sound of that voice was difficult to endure. She sat on a cowhide stool beside the cot; day and night, this was her post, her duty. Bowie brushed aside her words, her hand.

"I'll do as I like—still alive. What news, Kenly?"

"Not so bad." Kenly smiled cheerfully and patted the rifle he bore. It was Jim Bowie's rifle, turned over to him with hearty handclasp. "This pill-thrower of yours is running Crockett close. He got seven today, you got five, by my hand. They don't have the stomach for close grips. Those nearer batteries pay dear for every shot they throw into us."

"Damn it, can't see plain," rasped Bowie. "Those thirty— Mexicans still out there—where they tried to bridge the river?"

"Most of them," and Kenly nodded. "And plenty more with 'em."

"Good. If—if I could only—point a rifle. A damned hulk! Hundred and eighty men—to hold off thousands—do our best."

"Hugo, you must go, go!" urged Josefa. Her face was white. Her eyes, twin pools of light, were wistful and anxious. Yet they were serene, with the strange calm look that had settled in the faces of so many men in this place. "It exhausts him, this talking."

"Must have—news," came the deathly whisper. "Any word— from Fannin?"

"No. Travis has sent off the last call," Kenly replied. "He says if any reinforcements were coming, they'd have been here by this time. Probably Fannin can't get through with his four hundred men."

Bowie shook with a harsh, shallow cough.

"Old woman politics. No sayso. Pull Dick, pull devil. Fight our own battles! We'll—we'll fight 'em."

In the dusk, Kenly went down the stairs, leaving Bowie to Josefa's care.

General Cos had well fortified all this place. Kenly came out in the large walled yard or plaza. He made his way around into the smaller enclosure, the horse cuartel in the rear of the barracks.

Here, as being in better shelter than elsewhere, were the supper fires of the men off guard duty. Here too were women, on their way to and from the chapel that housed them. Lieutenant Dickinson's wife, her babe in arms, Mexican women, loyal to their husbands—for there were Mexicans in the Alamo, as well as Americans.

A scene for an etcher. Rifles and muskets, haggard powder-smeared faces. Davy Crockett's coonskin cap, the beard of Travis fair in the firelight. Captain Ward the Irishman, jovial, but sworn to touch no liquor during the siege. Bonham from South Carolina, polished, high-tempered as a Toledo blade. Lieutenant Dickinson just in from posting guard, Captain Albert Martin the Indian fighter, to the succor with a hardy company from Gonzales. Firelight aglitter on stone walls, knives, powder horns.

The tricolor with its slogan of 1824 still waved above the chapel. The red flag still flew from San Fernando church. The Alamo had grimly outfaced another vicious deluge of shot and shell pouring in from dawn to dark, opening breaches, smashing walls. Rifle barrels were still uncooled, thumbs were blistered from the hot vents of cannon. Today, succeeding that hot bombardment, had been rather quiet, as though in sheer weariness of attack and defense. Yet the quiet held something ominous and sinister.

Reinforcements? Thirty-one men from Gonzales, under Martin, had broken through the lines in the night. Bonham, out on express service, had dashed in upon his creamy buckskin horse. El Colorado, the red-headed John W. Smith of Bejar, had been in and out, he was gone now on a last desperate appeal for aid. One hundred and eighty-three as Kenly counted them, actives. No more expected. The Mexicans had cut off the water supply. It was the fifth day of March.

FROM THE misty black sky the stars twinkled faintly.

From the darkened plain outside the walls, the wafted cries, repeated from point to point, of the Mexican pickets: "*Sentinela alerta!*" Out there, one approach unguarded, one way still open, perhaps to trick the defenders into leaving and catch them unwalled. Here, walls scarred by ball and shell, the main yard pitted by bursting iron. In this little court, the fires ruddily illumined the figures of squatting men, and with their altar flames set the shadows to dancing. The horses, behind their guard-rope, fidgeted.

As Kenly sat down, Crockett handed him a sizzling strip of beef skewered by ramrod spit, with a hearty word and jest.

"Work your jaws and you'll be as good as a congressman. Good thing we got a big hole in them walls. I'm lookin' for Santy Anny to come through. Once we tree him, if somebody'll pin back his ears and grease his head, I'll engage to swaller him horns and all."

There was a general laugh. Bonham turned to Kenly.

"How's Bowie?"

"Weaker. He says he'll hold out for the finish."

The gay, devil-may-care voice of Ward uplifted. "The finish, is it? That's what I'm holding out for myself, glory be! The sooner we finish this business, the sooner Jim Ward can be washing the dust from his gullet. Crockett, I'll guarantee to drink you under the table the day this is over and I can settle down for a bit of good honest drinking. What d'ye say?"

"Taken," and Crockett chuckled. "Santy Anny's got the b'ar by the tail. He has his choice of ends. Who was it said that a Texan army was a-coming if we held out for a spell?"

"Army be damned," said somebody. "There's only one man back yonder worth a damn, and that's Sam Houston. The rest of 'em's politicians."

"Hurray!" crowed Davy Crockett. "Boys, you never seen such ornery humans as them politicians—looks like they'd ought to be in jail and let the honest prisoners be turned loose."

"Thought you were a politician?" said Kenly. "In Congress, weren't you?"

"You bet," said Crockett. "In and out. I got in and was rascaled out. But I made 'em pay twenty-five dollars a vote to beat me! Yes, sir. They got Davy Crockett's hide, but they paid heavy for it. If I'd had one hundred and thirty votes more, I wouldn't have come to Texas to show you fellers how to aim a rifle."

So the talk ran on. The fires glowed and flickered, and sank to dulling coals. The shadows danced no more, but stole in nearer and closer. The men stretched out as they pleased, or sought sleeping quarters in chapel and barrack. Kenly, who had a blanket in the corner, stretched out.

A musket shot far in the night outside. Another. Warning, angry shouts from the Mexican pickets, post to post. Kenly sprang up; he did not know how long he had been asleep. Other men were up and about. These panicky shots in the night were nothing new, but nerves were frayed and twitched easily.

"Jabbering like donkeys they are," growled the voice of Ward. "Bad luck to the lot of 'em for spoiling my dreams!"

The shrill cries among the enemy outposts died away. Silence ensued. Sudden upon it burst forth hasty challenge from the Texan guarding the sally-port. "*Quien vive?* Halt or be damned, you—hey, Colonel Travis! Somebody come a-running!"

A mutter of parley, of excited voices, then the scuff of feet. Dim forms took body, a little group staggering into the court. The thud of a body dumped down beside a smouldering fire, embers kicked into a glow.

"Where's Colonel Travis? Here's a deserter or a messenger, dunno which. He talked English, all right."

Travis had come. The court was filling with a gathering of curious, grumbling men. The fire flamed up. The lax mass there upon the ground might once have been a man. It was only stuff of filthy rags, blood matted and flowing. Now the eyes came open, all bleared and questioning. They rested, with slow wonder, upon the uniform of Travis. A hand wavered up in salute with arm across chest, as the thing tried to sit up.

"Sergeant Devore, sir. Present and—and—"

Devore fell back. His eyes rolled, a noise was in his throat. Kenly knelt over him with a canteen, poured water between his lips.

"Devore! What is it? Where'd you come from?"

"Tomorrow Santy Anny—tomorrow—"

Devore's eyes bulged out, his voice failed. Then with a writhe and a great effort, he came half up again. "A bust! Double-shot the guns!" His voice suddenly rang forth. "Fix bayonets—here they come! Give 'em Gin'ral Jackson, boys—"

Smothered in a cough and a belch of crimson, the voice was gone. Devore was gone, with a sigh. He stretched out and the flow from his gunshot wounds ebbed.

"Ran the lines, eh?" said Travis. "Two of you men lift him away; we'll bury him in the morning. What was it he said, Kenly? Did he have a message?"

"I think he did," said Kenly grimly. "He couldn't get it out. Something about tomorrow. Not hard to guess what it might have been."

TRAVIS NODDED in silence, drowning down. Captain Ward put in his word.

"Double-shot the guns, is it? Begad, I'd like to see it done! Devil enough left for a decent load all around, let alone double-shooting them."

"Was he warning us of an assault, think you?" asked Bonham.

"Hardly likely," rejoined Travis, with a shake of the head. "They're sure of us; they want to wear us down, now that they've cut off our water supply. They'll be slow to face fourteen cannon and our rifles."

"Maybe; but if them yeller gentry ain't snooping 'round out thar in the dark, then I'm an Injun! Who was this feller?"

"A deserter from the army," said Kenly. "Deserted in New

Orleans and went into the Mexican service. I always thought him a blackguard and a scoundrel; but now I'm not so sure. Yes, he had a message, right enough."

"It's a pity dead men can't be living for the space of a little chat," said Ward, reflectively. "Tomorrow, eh? Bad luck to them if they bother us on a Sunday!"

"Bull fight day," said a voice somewhere in the darkness. "Bet a dollar that's the ticket, boys! It'd be like 'em to try and rush us tomorrow."

"They can't drive us out." The voice of Travis broke over the others; it was calm, quiet. His face lifted. "We've all agreed, no retreat and no surrender; they can kill us, but here we stay. Still, I'm holding no man here. It's possible to get away. Any who so wishes may take a horse and go. The Gonzales men got in. Bonham got in. Smith and others have gone. Perhaps they're going to draw in their lines tomorrow and surround the place completely with a ring of cannon. That might be what this man tried to tell us. Last chance, men! Anyone who wants—"

"Aw, hell! Nobody's going. Save your breath," piped up somebody. There was a general laugh. Devore's body was carried away. Travis and Bonham, talking earnestly together, departed, Crockett touched Kenly's arm.

"Dummed if I don't smell Injuns! Come along and take a prowl."

Kenly nodded. Together they sought the west wall of the shell-pitted plaza, peering out toward river and town. Men slept beside the guns. Sentinels were on the alert. Out there, all was mist and starlight and obscurity.

Straining his faculties, Kenly fancied he could catch a faint and eerie noise, a jingling, a measured but hushed stir of movement, from the damp murk shrouding the river crossing. But he could not be certain. Nor could Crockett.

"They might be as lively out yonder as a Dutch cheese in the dogdays," grumbled Crockett, "but this fix takes the eyes of an owl as well as the ears of an ass. Betsy and I will wait till morning."

They clambered down again. Kenly sought his blankets, but the brooding mystery of the night, the taut nerves of him, kept sleep afar for a little. Bowie—this man Devore vomiting vain words and dying upon suspicion of last gallantry—the strange stirring silence of the Mexican outposts and batteries—what next? But he himself was here now. The devil had been met and broken. He was here among men who made him hearty welcome. Here where he belonged, for good or ill—and so, the tension departed, he slept, and smiled as he slept. All the Alamo slept.

"Up, men, up! To your posts! They're coming!"

A grip on his shoulder, a quick voice above him. Kenly was up on the instant, snatching Bowie's rifle and his powder-horn. Then he was stumbling, running, weaving among the other men, across for the west wall where it loomed ghostly in the pale gray of early dawn. Excited voices were gasping hot words. The plaza was rife with dim figures bolting hither and thither.

AT THE wall now. Captain Ward was at the gun, mounted on its earthen platform midway of the wall; his gun crew were there, he was speaking sharply, coolly, gayly. Davy Crockett's figure loomed, peering forward like an Indian. "Betsy" ready in his hand. He welcomed Kenly with a grunt, no more.

The air was chill and thick. All sounds were muffled; but sounds there were, cautious, deliberate, as of a dragon-teeth host springing to life there in the obscurity. The darkness seemed to hold death in ambush. The hushed murmurs of men came from along the wall. The spark of the gunner's match was gently waving. Came the "tap-tap-tap" of ramrods shoving home down the line.

"Hooray for Jackson and New Orleans!" said Crockett abruptly. "If we ain't—"

The instant notes of an eager bugle sounded, repeated from point to point. A closer and higher cheer from many throats.

The flares of rockets showering the sky with abrupt fire. No further concealment now; forth came the slashing strains of a hundred brasses, the thunder of drums, and all was plain to see.

There across the plain beyond the wall, a bristling column of men, cheering, bent forward at the double, bursting forward like swimmers breasting shallow surf.

"Take 'em two in line," grunted Crockett coolly. "You can spit a hull file—"

"Here they are, boys! Give 'em hell!" That was the quick, high voice of Travis, beside the eight-pounder on the far right. Then came the thunderous explosion of Ward's gun, shaking the very wall. Grape hissed forth, and the storm-tools of the Mexican sappers were tossed above a swirl of plunging men, as the serried ranks were broken.

The gun beside Kenly exploded. The billow of smoke almost blocked his view; but now Crockett's rifle cracked. His own weapon was up; sights sought and found their mark, and came the recoil as he touched trigger. Then to reload swiftly, frantically.

Captain Ward was swearing mightily, his gun crew sponging and ramming like mad. Crockett was venting Indian warwhoops. All the stretch of wall gushed sulphur, cracked with fire of rifle and musket. The Alamo was a ring of gunfire, pouring death back upon the death that threatened.

In the turmoil and stress and uproar a man was two persons. Kenly, firing and reloading, firing again through the rifts in the smoke, was conscious of the things around. Crockett and his Indian whoops, Ward, furious and swearing; the reiterant voice of Travis pealing like a trumpet with its *No rendirse!* No surrender, boys!"

The yelling enemy in columns there below, assaulting like a shadowy sea rolling up from all quarters; up above, Josefa, wide-eyed above the cot of Jim Bowie, and below, the women crowded in the chapel, Mrs. Dickinson with her babe! Ah, for one glimpse of Santa Anna's black charger there, beyond his rifle sights!

The tumult waned, the streaming smoke-spurts paused and lifted upon the gray light. The air was pealing with frenzied cheers, with hysteric laughter. Hurrah! The columns out there had fled the blast. The ground was littered with dead and creeping things, with muskets, ladders and axes.

Broken ranks were jostling and thronging to rear, officers and men alike.

So much for this side—what of the north? By the excitement there, the most determined attack must have been launched at the breach—but it was clear, clear! Not an enemy was within the enclosure; they were in full retreat there. None had won in from the south either—cheers were rising on all sides. Smashed them!

Gunners were busy swabbing out pieces, stacking up the little stands of grape. Captain Ward was wiping his face and swearing exultantly. "By the saints, there's a Sunday sermon for 'em!" The wall was rimmed with the shapes of men jutting above the parapet; powder-grimed faces, blinking and squinting, while hands nervously hefted powder horn and cartridge boxes amid jeer and jest. Travis appeared beside his gun in the northwest embrasure which raked the breach. His voice lifted; Kenly heard it, cool and assured.

"They're coming, boys. *No rendirse!* No surrender!"

Coming? Kenly whirled. Yes, the ranks were reforming. The men along the wall settled lower, their long barrels fringing the parapet. The light was stronger now. He could recognize the troops forming up again—the Zapadores or engineers, the battalions of Toluca and Matamores—three columns of them preparing.

Then music outburst. The blaring bands of the enemy, massed beyond the river, lifted a monotonous and savage air; it was pitched to a wild note that stirred the passions like the impelling beat of a fandango.

"*El Deguello!*" exclaimed a Mexican in the battery near Kenly. "The Cutthroat—what is played always for the killing of the bull. It means no quarter, *hombres!*"

"We'll teach 'em the devil's jig instead," and Captain Ward laughed gayly.

Again, again! The flood broke forward. Kenly could look now only at the column spreading for this western wall. Crockett's voice jerked at him.

"Pick off the ladder men. I call the whiskers in the red cap."

Betsy cracked; whiskers dropped, self and ladder. "I win the beef!" and Crockett laughed as he rammed in his charge. Another man was at the ladder, lifting it. Kenly's bullet dropped him. Another reached for it; Crockett's bullet was first. Smoke rose in a cloud; from end to end the wall erupted bullets that tore through this veil.

BELOW, SPECTRAL figures were stumbling, running, crawling; the van of the column had turned in upon itself as though withered by a scorching gust. Yet this time it did not break. It won forward, under the walls, beyond the reach of the cannon. Part of it flooded away toward the north side, shrinking from grape and ball.

Brief pause as the din dwindled. The flag still flew, the second assault had been blunted—but louder, more insistent, swelled the infernal *Deguello.* The smoke hung in the moist spring air, the dawn-light was mounting into the sky. Blunted and beaten—

Oh! No! Everything was drowned by a tremendous uproar to the north, by rapid explosions. Bullets were volleying from the ranks below, searching out the parapet, the riflemen, the gunners. This was the death grapple. The wall there was enveloped in the smoke of cannon, rifle and musket. "No surrender, boys!" Travis stood by the corner gun, shouting—ah! Where was he? Gone. A trickle of Mexican uniforms poured in at the breach. The trickle widened. The dam burst. A torrent came rushing in. Under the cannon muzzles now, so that the men on the parapet fired straight down. Then the parapets were cleared, the outer works were taken. There was a rush of defenders for the barracks.

Kenly heard scrape of ladder poles, the scrape of feet. A swarthy, sweated visage rose on the ladder there. Kenly fired and the figure vanished, clearing the others below him from the ladder. But there were other ladders. In the powder haze glittered uniforms. Men were rising to swing clubbed rifles. Bullets whistled and screamed.

"Off out o' here 'fore we're treed!" shouted Crockett.

"Wait, wait! Lend a hand!" Captain Ward's cry rose with shrill insistence. He pointed at the flood bursting through. "Two stands o' shot left!"

The gun crew were tugging at the trunnion. Kenly and Crockett lent their weight to the blocked wheels, deeply sunk in the furrows of recoil; the piece was mounted on earth fills. They swung it about. A moment later, it roared forth a stand of grape into the crowded foe thronging the north enclosure.

Ward's yell of exultation rose shrill. "Again! Load!"

A hornet flight of musket balls, spatting against the gun, against flesh. Men fell. There beyond, Bonham was gone now, like Travis. A surge of Mexican soldiery was inside, the Texans retreating to the barracks. A man fell against Kenly, bullets thudding into him. Then Ward fired, and the grape mowed terribly into those crowded ranks.

"Jump for it!"

Crockett was gone, Kenly after him, the others, such as remained alive, followed. Down and making for the barracks. A wave of the enemy swept forward to cut them off ere they could reach it. But no—Ward had not followed! He was swinging a rammer, there on the parapet—Kenly had a brief glimpse of him, of bayonets flashing, a brief catch of his gay, wild cheer—

Then it was body against body, gun against gun, hand against bayonet. Kenly won through somehow, with Crockett, or almost through. Another flood surged forward; he had vision of a keen, dark face, a sword thrusting at him—Don Rodrigo, of all men! Recognition came to both, suddenly, in a flashing glimpse. Then Crockett's rifle fell and smashed, and Don Rodrigo was gone.

Through, through somehow, a handful of them. The doorways of the barracks row were spitting smoke. Kenly gained the south end room, with Crockett beside him. Their smashed rifles were replaced by others—no lack of them now. Overhead, Kenly knew, lay Jim Bowie, and Josefa was there; no matter for her now, let her go with the rest.

THROUGH THE smoke pierced the savage strains of the *Deguello*, over and over. The main battle had not started yet. The enemy had won the outer works, true, had silenced the cannon; but there remained the barracks row, with entrenched loopholes, with doorways, spitting Texan bullets. Here in the south room, the makeshift hospital, were sick and wounded, and a handful of others with Kenly and Crockett.

This whole barracks row commanded the outer works. The Texan rifles were speaking fast and furiously. Officers and men below were falling. The Mexicans wheeled around cannon and emptied them into the structure; they began to take the barracks room by room—pouring grape or ball into it, then charging.

Here in the south room, there was quick work—the sick and hurt could load, Kenly and Crockett and their men could fire. Quick and fast; the gold epaulettes died down below, until Crockett let out a yell.

"Watch out! The gun! Pick 'em off!"

Ward's gun was being worked around, loaded with solid ball. A howitzer was being wheeled forward for closer range; the rifles spoke out. Men died about the guns, but men were dying here, too. Crockett staggered, dropped his rifle; then he picked it up again and let out a war whoop as he passed it back for a fresh one. Blood was running down over his hand.

The cannon roared. There was a blast, a rocking burst of dust; the ball had torn clear through the corner wall, taking half of the south side away. Crockett whooped in derision, and fired on the men loading the howitzer. It was coming up point-blank for the door. Rifles and muskets were hot and fouled; bullets poured in by door and loophole, but still the Texan rifles cracked, rapidly, ever reloaded by the sick and hurt. The howitzer was loaded, a man leaped for it with the match. Crockett killed him. Another caught up the match—

"Look out, everybody!"

With the wild yell, Crockett leaped for cover. It was Kenly's last sight of him, though he heard the wild whoop once more from the stockade to the south. The howitzer roared. The entrenchment was fairly blown to fragments; the room was filled with grape, sweeping a devil's tattoo. Brains and flesh, dead and wounded. Still a rifle or two speaking. Kenly fired, fired again.

Once more the howitzer roared death into the room. Bloody bayonets flooded into the doorway, dark faces with them. Kenly flung himself at them like a madman, swinging the barrel of his rifle. No stock left; the iron swung horribly, crunched as it fell. They broke before him and the others with him. Then they came flooding in again.

Somehow, he knew not how, Kenly was on the stairs now. The thought of Josefa drew him despite bayonet and ball. Confusion and smoke and dust, and corpses underfoot. Then he was out of it all, out into peace and quiet above, and the silent room where Jim Bowie lay.

Kenly staggered in. The iron fell from his hand. He leaned against the wall, gulping air into his lungs. Josefa caught him; there was a taste of blood in his mouth. He could not speak or move. Before him the eyes of Bowie glittered cold and grim, the two pistols waited their prey. His knuckles were white on the grips. His horrible voice rasped out faint words.

"Get out—of the way."

Josefa pulled Kenly from the doorway. He tried to pick up the rifle-barrel and could not. He pitched forward on his knees, hearing Josefa's cry at his ear, feeling her arms about his neck. Hit, of course; no telling where. He was helpless. Blood was soaking his shirt. Josefa was tearing at it, ripping it away. Blood dribbled into his eyes.

Then the feet on the stairs. The infernal bedlam had quieted into scattering shots. The blare of the *Deguello* lifted triumphant. Shouts and shots came from the chapel below, no more. Quick spasmodic cries. And the strange protective silence of this alcoved room above was being broken now. Shadows darkened the doorway. A face was thrust forward, drawn back again. Kenly tried to rise, saw Bowie's eyes fastened on the door, saw the brief, grim smile on those death-marked lips. Then he pitched forward on his face, with Josefa trying desperately to hold him.

"Muerte! A la muerte!" The brisk order outside: to the death! Bayonets leaped in the doorway. Men burst forward there. The lifted pistols spoke out. Bodies fell; fell upon Josefa and upon Kenly as he lay unconscious. Blood flowed along the floor. The knife in Bowie's hand was flashing now. A crash of a musket, then another. The bayonets suddenly grew bold and greedy. They flickered down at the cot. The knife rose and fell, and the bayonets rose red.

Men yelled and shouted exultantly. The dead thing was lifted from the bed and stripped. Bayonets lifted it; upon bayonets it was lifted and passed and riddled, out and down the stairs, to be thrown among the others there and riddled anew. And after it poured the men—those that were left of them.

The massed brasses no longer blared their *Deguello* strain; they had ceased, crescendo. The smoke of battle had eddied away before the first breeze, venturing upon the scene like the breath of a timid spring. The sky was brightened for the coming of the tardy, regretful sun. And yet, not an hour had elapsed since the token of the bugles and the rockets, and the first tempestuous bars of the *Deguello.*

WHIMPERINGS, GROANS, anguished cries began to resound, everywhere. A white face, streaked with blood, lifted in the alcoved room above. Josefa, on hands and knees, then rising, shivering, her eyes dilating upon the dead men. She dropped again and her hands sought Kenly's head, his heart.

Suddenly she sprang up, she stood listening. Voices rose from below, laughing voices. Some sick men still alive were being dragged out. A quick, sharp order, a silence, then a ragged volley. Pale as death, she looked down at Kenly, and shivered.

Her gaze caught one of those who had first fallen. An officer, to whom one of those pistols had brought the end of earthly things. Josefa stifled a sharp cry, then fell upon him avidly. Something struck her hand; it was the great knife, silvered shaft sticky with blood. She caught at it. In a moment she had freed the dead man's braided jacket and was drawing it upon the limp, unresistant torso of Kenly. The wound there was ragged, but by no means bad. Another above his eyes, where a spent ball had landed and drawn blood. It was disfiguring; her lips brushed the poor hurt face. Then she got the jacket on him, caught up a red cap and jammed it over his head.

Now what—now what? She stood up panting, desperate. Voices reached her from below; the voices of Mexican women. She turned and went outside.

She could see them there, being led forth out of their huddled refuge in the bloody chapel, nine or ten of them. An American woman, Señora Dickinson. But no child now; the child lay with the father. Just the woman. Her eyes roved about. Search parties were lifting out wounded Mexicans, jabbing red bayonets into any Texans who still lived. One of these parties caught her attention, one figure leading them. The name leaped to her lips.

"Pablo! Oh, Pablo!"

The pock-marked face looked up. Pablo saw her.

Late night; dawn an hour away. A shielded candle threw stealthy glow. It dwelt on the pock-marked face of Pablo, the anxious loveliness of Josefa, the hard bandaged visage of Kenly, whose eyes glittered from beneath the bloody cloth. The hut was empty except for these three. Other huts around, here between town and Alamo, echoed moaning voices, the irritant cries of wounded men.

"Among the wounded, eh?" said Kenly. He understood now. "Thanks, my friend; thanks. And you?"

"I stay," said Pablo. The stolid man was broken. Nerves shattered, a febrile hurry in his eyes and voice. He leaned forward, muttering swiftly.

"I have a horse ready. You must do it now or never. You and she both. With dawn it is too late. Wood has been gathered day and night; they are moving out the wounded, tearing down these huts. The bodies are to be burned; the Texan bodies. It is an insult, as one burns dogs. Our own dead will be buried. All are dead. If you're able to ride—"

"I'm able," said Kenly shortly. "Sentries?"

"There are none here. I can take you out, see you off. In another hour—"

"Do it, then. Help me up."

KENLY STOOD on his feet. He was stiff and sore and weak; shattered outside and in, but it must be done. Josefa's arm was in his.

One horse, and enough. It was Spanish custom for a lady to ride in front, sideways upon the lap of her cavalier. Josefa laughed a little hysterically under her breath as she settled into place. A handgrip with stout Pablo in the darkness; then off.

Silence; the clod-clod of the horse heading into the northeast, following the unguarded road. Faces to the dawn, the first twitter of birds lifting among the trees. The movement hurt, but Kenly set his teeth grimly. After a long while Josefa broke the silence.

"It shall be for Texas, then?"

"For Texas," Kenly echoed. "And forever, my heart."

The sun streaked the east red and gold. They halted. Kenly drew rein, white and haggard, at limit of endurance. The sunlit warmth of morning was grateful. He slid to the ground, tore

off the braided jacket and dropped it with a gesture of abhor-
rence.

Then he sat staring at the sky. Peace ruled the deep blue and
the greening earth. The hand of Josefa crept into his and he
gripped it hard. She was pointing. From their height, there was
a red dot that punctuated the horizon—the flag still floating
from the church of San Fernando. And, against it, blotting it
out, lifted a long pillar of smoke and then another, floating
straight up into the sky.

"The burning," said Josefa, and shuddered. "Dead, all dead."

"No!" Kenly drew a deep breath. His head came up. "Not
dead; never that. What of it? Death is only the beginning, my
heart. The beginning for them, for us, for everything; the beginning, always! Life's dead behind us, yours and mine. We begin
again, you and I, together. For them—yes, for them, too, life
begins. Texas begins. Wait! You'll see. Texas is born—"

His voice failed and died. After a time she spoke softly, as
Kenly's hand caressed her slim cheek.

"Here, Hugo; look at it. I think Don Santiago must be glad
now that we have it again. See how bright the handle and the
blade! Take it, as a gift from him; for after all, he thought well
of you." She thrust the knife upon Kenly, then looked up into
his eyes, questioningly. "Do you think they'll burn Don Santiago, too? Surely not. He was too brave a man—"

Far away the words were echoed, where *El Presidente* General
Don Antonio Lopez Benemerito de Santa Anna was looking
down upon a stripped and bayonet-slashed lump of clay. Hes-
itation came upon him.

"Too brave a man to meet the fate of a dog," he muttered.
He looked at the blazing sacrificial pyres; of the bodies there,
by record, were *ciento ochenta y tres*—a hundred and eighty-three.
Then he shrugged and turned away.

"No matter! No matter!" he said carelessly, "Throw him in."

H. BEDFORD-JONES

BEDFORD-JONES IS a Canadian by birth, but not by profession, having removed to the United States at the age of one year. For over twenty years he has been more or less profitably engaged in writing and traveling. As he has seldom resided in one place longer than a year or so and is a person of retiring habits, he is somewhat a man of mystery; more than once he has suffered from unscrupulous gentlemen who impersonated him—one of whom murdered a wife and was subsequently shot by the police, luckily after losing his alias.

The real Bedford-Jones is an elderly man, whose gray hair and precise attire give him rather the appearance of a retired foreign diplomat. His hobby is stamp collecting, and his collection of Japan is said to be one of the finest in existence. At present writing he is en route to Morocco, and when this appears in print he will probably be somewhere on the Mojave Desert in company with Erle Stanley Gardner.

Questioned as to the main facts in his life, he declared there was only one main fact, but it was not for publication; that his life had been uneventful except for numerous financial losses, and that his only adventures lay in evading adventurers. In his younger years he was something of an athlete, but the encroachments of age preclude any active pursuits except that of motoring. He is usually to be found poring over his stamps, working at his typewriter, or laboring in his California rose garden, which is one of the sights of Cathedral Cañon, near Palm Springs.

Bedford-Jones has written stories laid in many corners of the earth, but among his most popular tales were the John Solomon stories which started many years ago in the *Argosy*.